# American Boy

—◦—

Also by Larry Watson

*In a Dark Time*
*Leaving Dakota*
*Montana 1948*
*Justice*
*White Crosses*
*Laura*
*Orchard*
*Sundown, Yellow Moon*

# American Boy

## Larry Watson

milkweed
editions

The characters and events in this book are fictitious. Any similarity to real persons, living or dead, is coincidental and not intended by the author.

© 2011, Text by Larry Watson

Published 2011 by Milkweed Editions
Printed in Canada by Friesens Corporation
Cover design by Christian Fuenfhausen
Cover photo © Karen Hunnicutt Meyer. Reproduced with permission from the artist.
Author photo by Susan Watson
Interior design by Connie Kuhnz
The text of this book is set in Warnock Pro
11 12 13 14 15   5 4 3 2 1
*First Edition*

Please turn to the back of this book for a list of the sustaining funders of Milkweed Editions.

Library of Congress Cataloging-in-Publication Data

Watson, Larry, 1947–
American boy / Larry Watson. — 1st ed.
      p.    cm.
    ISBN 978-1-57131-078-1 (acid-free paper)
    1. Life change events—Fiction.   2. Small cities—Fiction.
  3. Minnesota—Fiction.   4. Psychological fiction.   I. Title.
    PS3573.A853A83 2011
    813'.54—dc23

                                        2011021334

This book is printed on acid-free paper.

To Susie

# American Boy

*I WAS SEVENTEEN YEARS OLD when I first saw a woman's bare breasts, in itself an unremarkable occurrence. But when you consider that I also saw my first bullet wound on that same body, you have a set of circumstances truly rare. And if the boy standing beside me that day had not already been as close as a brother, the experience would have bound us to each other in a way even blood would find hard to match.*

*We were exposed to these phenomena in order that we might learn something, but then the lessons we learn are not always those we are taught. . . .*

## 1.

ON THANKSGIVING DAY IN 1962 I was seated at the dining room table with the Dunbar family, father and mother, eight-year-old twins Janet and Julia, and Johnny, who was my age. In fact, there were people in Willow Falls, Minnesota, who believed that the Dunbars had two sets of twins, so inseparable were Johnny and I. That one of us was dark and the other fair, one taller and one slighter, wouldn't necessarily have dissuaded anyone from that belief; after all, sturdy Janet was blond and waifish Julia brunette. And since I walked in and out of the Dunbar house as I pleased, why wouldn't someone assume that Johnny and I shared a last name?

But I was a Garth, an outsider, though this was genially ignored by the Dunbars. A few years earlier, when Miss Crane assigned *Wuthering Heights* to our eighth-grade English class, I was among the few who read the novel with interest. I identified with Heathcliff, not only because his brooding, headstrong character reminded me of my own, but also because I, too, had been welcomed into a prosperous, loving family. In fact, if my waking hours could have been totaled up, they likely would have revealed that I spent more time at the Dunbar house than I did at my own.

Where, incidentally, a holiday meal was not being served. My mother worked as a waitress at Palmer's Supper Club, and Sam Palmer always remained open on holidays for the few customers who didn't care to cook for themselves. Before she left for work she'd said she was sorry and offered to cook a turkey another time, just for the two of us, but I waved off her apology. She couldn't afford to pass up the hours.

Besides, I was right where I wanted to be, sitting at the long mahogany table, candlelit and covered for the occasion with a linen tablecloth, and set with the dishes and silverware that appeared only on holidays. Despite the table's ample proportions, there was not enough room for all the food Mrs. Dunbar had prepared. On the sideboard waited apple and pumpkin pies, an extra bowl of stuffing, a basket of rolls, and a sweet potato casserole. The meal would be wonderful, of that I was certain. Mrs. Dunbar was an excellent cook, a woman who took more delight in the preparation of food than its consumption.

Dr. Dunbar had just finished carving the turkey—repeating in the process the joke he made every year about how his surgical training finally came in handy—when the doorbell chimed. Calling uninvited on Thanksgiving generally would have been perceived as rude in Willow Falls, but not at the Dunbar home.

A few of the older people in the community still referred to the Dunbars' grand Victorian mansion on the edge of town as the Gardiner place, after the wealthy merchant who built the house early in the twentieth century.

But shortly after moving in, Dr. Dunbar had an addition built onto the house, and it was there that he practiced with George McLaughlin, the doctor who took the young Rex Dunbar into his practice, bringing the Dunbars to Willow Falls. Initially the doctors kept their offices downtown, on the second floor of the building that had Karlsson's law firm and Burke's Pharmacy on the first, but once the new addition was completed, they moved into the Dunbars' house, along with Betty Schaeffer, their nurse-receptionist. Patients who required treatment beyond what doctors Dunbar, McLaughlin, or the four doctors in the Cumberland Clinic could provide had to travel fifty miles to the nearest hospital, which was located in Bellamy, Minnesota. Not until 1976 would Willow Falls have its own hospital, though the project had been proposed and debated for decades.

Because of Dr. McLaughlin's age, Dr. Dunbar handled the more difficult cases, performed all the surgery, and put in the longest hours. But he did so without complaint, and if someone rang the bell, even on Thanksgiving Day, Dr. Dunbar would never consider not answering the call of duty. It might be Mr. Kolshak, clutching a hand that required stitches because the knife slipped when he was carving the turkey. Or it might be Mrs. Shea, hoping that the doctor could come and take a look at her father, who had hurt his back shoveling the snow that drifted over Willow Falls the previous night. In any case, it was unlikely that someone would intrude on the Dunbars' holiday for any reason but an emergency.

Nevertheless, after rising to his feet, Dr. Dunbar paused. He lifted his pocket watch from his vest, snapped it open, and gazed at it almost as if he were posing. Dr. Dunbar was a

charming, confident man, and an imposing physical speci-
men. He was movie-star handsome—heavy browed and
square jawed—and his wavy black hair was combed back
tight to his skull. Amid his large features, his pencil-thin
mustache was almost lost. He was six foot three, broad
shouldered and barrel chested, and he moved in a way that
suggested power and self-assurance. He was an impeccable
dresser and he favored three-piece suits, which he purchased in Minneapolis.

Dr. Dunbar placed his watch back into his vest pocket,
smiled apologetically at all of us sitting around the table,
and excused himself. Because we all knew that there had
to be an emergency, and because Dr. Dunbar's departure
inevitably meant that the room lost its energy, we waited
in silence for his return.

Alice Dunbar was her husband's opposite—shy, timid,
and tiny. She was, however, his match in looks—a fair-
haired, fine-featured beauty. When they were together
in public, someone would inevitably remark on what an
attractive couple the Dunbars made, and how obvious it
was, from the way she gazed up at him, that Alice Dunbar
adored her husband. In fact, her need for him was such
that even ordinary moments could be difficult for her to
manage without his direction and vigor. And so when the
doctor left to answer the door, Mrs. Dunbar did nothing to sustain or stimulate the conversation. She just sat
there patiently fingering the pearls of her necklace, as if
counting them could substitute for counting the minutes
of his absence.

He came back wearing a somber expression. "That was

Deputy Greiner." As if he needed to assess each of our ability to endure his forthcoming announcement, the doctor looked around the table. He didn't pause long when he came to me. He knew I wouldn't flinch.

"There's been a shooting," the doctor went on. "The victim is a young woman by the name of Lindahl. Louisa Lindahl?"

The name was not familiar to any of us, so Dr. Dunbar continued. "According to the deputy, it's a strange situation. A man has confessed to the shooting and turned himself in, but we don't have a victim."

Dr. Dunbar paused again. "Here's what the deputy told me. Miss Lindahl and her boyfriend—Lester Huston? That name mean anything? No? Anyway, this young couple had a quarrel, and it was heated, so heated that Huston took a shot at Miss Lindahl. He claims he was provoked, that she threw a soup can at him. And here's the part I'm not clear on: Either Miss Lindahl tried to run away from him and he fired at her as she was fleeing, or he fired at her and then she ran. Whatever the case, she got away, but there is no doubt in Mr. Huston's mind that he shot her. Deputy Greiner is convinced of this as well, and not only because people don't turn themselves in for crimes they didn't commit. He also found corroborating evidence. Huston was living in a shack on this side of Frenchman's Forest, and when the deputy visited the scene he saw some blood on the ground. Greiner tried to follow the blood trail, but he lost it in the woods. Then he came here. He wanted me to know that Miss Lindahl is likely still out there bleeding from a gunshot wound. Or—and we certainly have to consider this possibility—she might be dead already. And now I need to decide whether to stay put, ready to treat this young woman in case they bring her here, or to join the deputy and the other men he's rounded up for the search party. That way I could be right there to treat her in the field."

Once again the doctor surveyed the table, looking steadily at each of us in turn. Dr. Dunbar was not a weak or indecisive man, and it was unlikely that he was actually seeking counsel. As it was, Dr. Dunbar had already gone beyond what most fathers would have done. In that time and place—a small Midwestern town buttoned up tight with the early sixties' sense of decorum—few fathers would have shared these details with their family, much less asked for advice. A few heads of households might have called their wives aside and apprised them of the situation, but to involve the children was almost unheard of.

Nevertheless, I offered an opinion, which was testimony to my brashness rather than to any wisdom or practical judgment I might have possessed. "You could stay here," I suggested, "and Johnny and I could try to help find her."

"Well, there's an idea. And not a bad one," Dr. Dunbar said. "Well? Anyone else want to weigh in? Either in favor of Matthew's proposal or not."

Since I had volunteered Johnny for duty, I expected that he might speak up.

"No?" the doctor said. Then, to my surprise, he added, "All right then. We have a plan."

The creases that appeared between Mrs. Dunbar's eyes led me to believe that she didn't agree, but she said nothing.

"I know you fellows are hungry," Dr. Dunbar said, taking

in the meal spread before us, "but if you want to join the search party out at Frenchman's Forest, you'll have to head out right away. Time is not on the side of someone bleeding from a bullet wound."

Janet popped up out of her chair and asked, "Can we go, too?" Julia, often willing to allow her more vocal sister to speak for her, eagerly nodded her interest as well. The Dunbar twins were bright, bold little girls whose adventurous spirits made them seem more like their father than their mother.

Dr. Dunbar looked from one daughter to the other as if their request warranted serious consideration. Finally he said, "I don't doubt that you two have eyes every bit as sharp as the boys', but that's just the problem. I'm afraid you might find her. And that means you might see something you wish you hadn't. No, let's leave this one to the boys."

The twins looked both disappointed and relieved.

Johnny and I stood up and left the table in order to prepare for our expedition. While we put on our stocking caps, coats, and overshoes, Mrs. Dunbar assured us that a hot meal would be waiting when we returned. We were almost out the door when Dr. Dunbar called us aside.

"Now, if you do find her," he said, "don't try to do anything heroic." He handed each of us a stack of gauze pads. "A bullet wound is nothing to fool with. If she's bleeding heavily, use simple compression. No tourniquets or anything extreme." And then he added with a smile, "And absolutely no field surgery—don't dig out the bullet with a jackknife or anything along those lines. If you have to touch a wound, use the gauze, not your bare hands. Now go. I'll set up an emergency room in the clinic."

As we dressed to go out, Johnny and I were excited, almost giddy, at the prospect of adventure. But when we finally left the house we were solemn and subdued, mindful that the gauze in our pockets was meant to soak up human blood.

## 2.

IN THE STATE THAT BOASTED OF HAVING ten thousand lakes, Willow Falls was near none of them. Located in the southwestern corner of Minnesota, our town was closer to Sioux Falls, South Dakota, than it was to Minneapolis. We were out on the prairie, the land flat or gently undulating, sparsely populated, and mostly plowed for farming. As for recreation, the grassland was good for upland game, and a few nearby potholes and sloughs attracted wild fowl and the men who hunted them, but we were not a region of cabins on the lake. We did have a river, of course, the Willow, on whose banks the town was built. But it slowed to a trickle in dry years—of which there were many—and its falls, which gave the town its name, were in fact little more than a series of steps the river took as it stumbled over rocks and boulders near the center of town.

And if neither river nor falls merited their names, the same was true of our forest. In that part of Minnesota, only by an occasional stand of cottonwood and bur oak was the prairie interrupted—and then buckthorn, juneberry, and golden currant bushes filled in some open spaces along the river. It was a combination of these that made up

Frenchman's Forest, and without historical incident—in the nineteenth century, a trapper apparently hid in the undergrowth in order to escape a Sioux war party—the area probably never would have been named.

Frenchman's Forest was on the north edge of town, about a mile from the Dunbars'. We could have walked it, but since time was crucial Johnny drove his father's black Chrysler Imperial. And once we entered the forest we had no trouble finding Lester Huston's shack; we just followed the tracks made by other vehicles in the fresh snow.

Deputy Greiner and his search party were back at the site as well, ten men walking in slow, ever-widening circles, searching for any trace of a trail that would lead them to the victim. We climbed out of the Chrysler, but before we could get started, Tiny Goetz drove up in his old Chevy truck and loudly announced from the driver's seat that footprints, and perhaps blood as well, had been found along the road on the other side of the woods. With that news, the group immediately redirected their search. But Johnny and I declined to join them. We'd already decided to focus on the terrain most familiar to us—the overgrown paths and twisting trails of Frenchman's Forest.

Before the deputy and his men climbed into their cars, Johnny said, "Wait—shouldn't you give us a description of the woman?"

Deputy Greiner, a lean, perpetually sour-faced man who wore the same greasy fedora no matter the season, replied caustically: "I'll tell you what: if you come across a woman and she ain't been shot—you got the wrong woman."

Johnny thanked the deputy, but I knew that if Dr. Dunbar had been there, Greiner never would have spoken to him like that.

Also among the searchers was Ed Fields, my fifth-grade Sunday school teacher, and I asked him where the blood had been discovered. He pointed to a break in the woods near a fallen tree, and then he drove off with the deputy and the other men, their vehicles bumping along the snowy ruts of the unpaved road.

Even without Mr. Fields's direction, Johnny and I could have found the blood simply by going to the spot where the snow was packed down. We stood where the searchers had, looking down at two or three smears, the blood's crimson diluted in the snow. By then it was apparent that we wouldn't be able to follow the Lindahl woman's actual footsteps, because the other searchers had tracked up the snow completely.

Johnny and I entered Frenchman's Forest slowly, looking not for footprints, but rather another red stain in the snow. In the woods there was less snow but more debris—fallen branches and leaves and undergrowth—and these made for slow going.

Not having discussed a strategy, we each began to search in our own way. Johnny moved rapidly through the woods, hopping over branches and zigzagging through the brush in an effort to cover as much territory as possible. I kept my head down and determinedly trod through the leaves, deadfall, and thorny stalks of weeds.

Only nineteen days separated Johnny and me in age, but I often felt like his older brother, his worldly, rougher-edged older brother. I might have had access to the privileged world of the Dunbars, but at the end of the day I returned to the gloomy little two-bedroom box where I lived with my mother. We weren't exactly poor, but poverty was always within view. We often ate as well as the

Dunbars, but only because my mother brought leftovers home from work. And I seldom sat down to one of our warmed-over meals without wondering about its origins. Had Judge Barron sent that steak back because it was too well done? Was this baked potato originally placed in front of Doris Crum, the wife of Dr. Crum, the dentist? Did George Dummett, owner of Dummett's Hardware, touch this piece of chicken before pushing his plate aside?

But Johnny Dunbar wasn't only sheltered by his family's means; he was like a child in no hurry to grow up. Every initiation, every marker of adulthood that I couldn't wait for—smoking, drinking, driving, earning money, having sex, being independent—Johnny seemed in no hurry to reach. And what interest he had could often be satisfied vicariously by hearing of my exploits or efforts. If I was occasionally less than forthcoming about what Debbie McCarren and I were doing in her basement, or in the backseat of my mother's DeSoto, it was because Johnny's probing questions could be invasive. And if I indulged in a cigar or a six-pack of Hamm's, I didn't necessarily want to explain every sensation to him. After Randy Wadnor and I got into a scuffle at a football game, to take one example, I wanted to put the incident behind me as quickly as possible. Johnny, on the other hand, wanted to know every detail of the altercation. We both enjoyed sports, but Johnny was not competitive—he only wanted to play. And we were both good students, but while I studied to improve my future prospects, his success in school was the result of the wide-eyed curiosity he brought to any subject.

Johnny even looked like a little brother. He had his

father's curls, but he couldn't tame them. They frizzed and coiled in every direction, often making him look as if he'd just climbed out of bed. I could have grown a full beard at that age, while Johnny's cheeks produced nothing but down. The muscles of his slender body were smooth and undefined as well, and he had a childish habit of bouncing and squirming if he had to sit in one place for long. If anyone in town did believe we were brothers, they likely would have assumed that Johnny took after our delicate mother.

Johnny stopped abruptly ten yards ahead of me in the woods, and when I looked questioningly in his direction, he smiled and pointed up at the low branch of a tilting oak tree.

Many of the boys in our town—and even a few of the girls—grew up in these woods. We built forts, played hide-and-seek, climbed trees, and hunted, first with slingshots and BB guns, then with .22s. We formed clubs that had their headquarters in the forest, and we took refuge here when we needed to be alone with our sadness, confusion, or anger. Among these trees we hid from bullies and parents and authorities. We also went to Frenchman's Forest when we wanted to smoke cigarettes or drink the liquor we had stolen. A few of us had our first sexual experiences in here as well, and though that wasn't true for Johnny or for me, we both received a rudimentary sexual education in the forest years earlier, when Lannie Corbis straddled the branch of the very oak tree Johnny was standing under now, solemnly holding forth on the mechanics of sex to an eager but skeptical audience of five younger boys. Eventually we'd learn that Lannie was mistaken about some of the ways men and women fit together, but even the corrected record could not alter for me the association of sex with the smell of tree sap and the hum of insects.

"Lannie?" I said.

Johnny nodded, smiling.

Yes, if Louisa Lindahl was in these woods, we were the ones to find her. And it was not hard to imagine that someone fleeing a man with murderous intent would head for Frenchman's Forest.

We walked on, down through the treeless depression we called the Boulders, past the spot where Russell Marsh blasted an owl out of a hollow tree with a twelve-gauge, leaving nothing of the bird but a blizzard of feathers, and through the stand of willows whose wandlike limbs we used to swing from. As we searched for Louisa Lindahl, Johnny and I were the source of most of the noise in the forest—twigs snapping, leaves crunching, and clumps of snow falling, brushed from branches and shrubs.

Then I heard something, and I shushed Johnny. We both stopped and stood unmoving, our heads raised as if, like hounds, we could detect scents in the chilly air. We stood there for a moment, breathless.

After a long silence, Johnny whispered, "What was it?"

"I'm not sure."

"She could be hiding. For all she knows Lester Huston is out here looking for her."

I hadn't thought of that. I'd assumed she would want to be found.

Johnny asked, "Should we call out or something?"

Before I could form a judgment, Johnny cupped his hands to his mouth and shouted, "We're here to help you! Is anyone out there?"

When no response came, he tried again. "Hello! There's no need to be afraid!"

After the sound of Johnny's voice died away, the forest's silence seemed amplified, a snowy day's version of an echo.

"That's just what someone who's after her would say," I offered with a smile. "'There's no need to be afraid.'"

"What should I say—'Ollie, Ollie, in-free? Come out, come out, wherever you are?'"

Once we stood there motionless for a couple minutes, the cold was able to wrap itself around us. I clapped my gloved hands together and stamped my feet. "Jesus. If she's hiding in here, she could freeze to death."

Johnny pinched snot from his nostrils with his mitten. "Freeze or bleed to death. Some choice."

"Well, I don't think she'd *choose* either one."

"Smart-ass. Maybe I should howl like a wolf," he suggested. "Scare her out of hiding."

"Give it a try."

But he didn't. And both of us just stood there listening. After another moment, Johnny asked, "Could it have been a squirrel?"

"It wasn't like that. Not scurrying. More like starting and stopping. Like someone limping maybe. Or hunkering down in the leaves."

After a few more minutes passed, I began to convince myself that it must have been a squirrel I'd heard. Or possibly a branch, falling by stages from the top of a tall cottonwood. Then I heard it again. And this time Johnny did, too. It sounded like something scuffing slowly through the dry leaves, and we both turned around in the direction from which it came.

Why had that antlered buck not been frightened into flight? Had he sensed all along that we were no threat, clumping through the forest unarmed? Had he seen us for what we were, boys pretending that they knew his territory as well as he did, boys who thought they had powers greater than men? The buck stared at us and we stared at him for one more long moment, and then he moved on, pausing every few paces to scrape at the leaves in search of food, a being with a real purpose in the woods.

I looked down. If I hadn't been standing in snow the outline of my foot would have been hard to see. In late November, cold and snow hastened days to a close early in our part of the world, limiting what could be usefully done with the hours. And in the thickening gloom of Frenchman's Forest, it was already too dark to find footprints or traces of blood.

"We should probably head back," I said in the reluctant voice of a sensible big brother.

"And just leave her out here?"

"We don't even know that she's still out here."

"We don't know she isn't."

"Come on. In a few minutes we won't be able to see our hands in front of our faces."

Johnny kicked back and forth in the snow, perhaps testing my theory.

After another moment, he conceded. "All right."

As we walked back to the car, I felt discouraged and even humiliated. We had set out with a mission and an accompanying sense of importance, but it seemed most likely that no one, and certainly not Dr. Dunbar, had ever believed we had a realistic chance of finding Louisa

Lindahl. It felt now as if our expedition had merely been allowed, indulged as the behavior of children is indulged. *Let them go; what's the harm?* And now, like children, we were coming in from our play when darkness fell.

## 3.

UPON RETURNING TO THE DUNBAR HOUSE, our senses were immediately assaulted. Though the meal had been prepared hours earlier, the aroma of stuffed turkey and pumpkin pie lingered, as inseparable from the house as its warmth from fire and furnace. Then Janet came bounding toward us shouting, "She's here! She's here!"

"Who's here?" Johnny asked.

"The shot girl!"

Julia ran into the room just in time to correct her sister. "The girl who got shot!"

Mrs. Dunbar hurried close behind, trying to quiet the girls. But their excitement had them bouncing in place.

"Mom?" said Johnny, "what are they talking about?"

Mrs. Dunbar put her finger to her lips, as if to indicate that even his question was too loud. "They brought her here shortly after you left," she whispered.

Johnny and I looked at each other, trying to comprehend what we'd just been told. It felt almost as if we were the victims of a practical joke.

The snow we'd stamped from our boots hadn't even melted when Dr. Dunbar entered the room. "Well boys, sorry if your search was for naught." He was still wearing the vest and tie he'd had on at the dining room table, but he'd exchanged his suit coat for a white lab coat.

"She's here?" Johnny asked again.

"She is indeed."

"How is she?" I asked. "Is she . . . ?"

"She's seen better days, I promise you that. But all in all, she's faring pretty well." He was smoking a cigarette, but he'd only taken a couple drags. He handed it now to Mrs. Dunbar, who smoked Chesterfields as did the doctor, but she held the cigarette as if she wasn't quite sure what to do with it. "In fact," he added, "I should probably get back in there. She'll be coming around soon."

As he turned to walk back through the house to the clinic, something came over me. I don't really remember deciding to follow the doctor, but follow I did, as surely as if I'd been invited.

Johnny trailed along as well, but to this day I believe he was following me and not his father.

Dr. Dunbar had not gone far before he realized he was being shadowed. He slowed and looked back over his shoulder. "Yes?"

Mrs. Dunbar had also joined our little entourage, but all of us stopped now, and we stood in a small, dimly lit parlor. Back in the bright foyer, the twins were still spinning with excitement.

"What is it?" the doctor asked. I had no doubt that his question was directed to me.

I had no reply.

"Would you like to see the patient?"

Of course I wanted to see the patient, but Dr. Dunbar knew this about me before I knew it myself.

"Oh, Rex," said Mrs. Dunbar, "do you think that's a good idea?"

"Let's leave it up to them. If they'd rather not, that's just fine as well." He turned to us. "Well?"

I was instantly ready to say yes, but I knew Johnny had to answer first.

"Is she . . . okay?" he asked.

Dr. Dunbar reached inside the sleeve of his white coat and readjusted a cuff link. "She is now," he said succinctly. "Or will be soon enough."

"All right," said Johnny, looking at me. "Sure." Apprehension flickered in his eyes. He might have hoped I'd say that I wasn't interested, but there was no chance of that.

"Very well then," Dr. Dunbar said. "Let's see if I can teach you something about the treatment of bullet wounds."

As odd as this situation might seem, there was reason and precedent behind it. Both Johnny and I had expressed an interest in medicine as a career. Dr. Dunbar hadn't prodded us in that direction, but since he made every endeavor—from casting a spinner into the river to manipulating a dislocated shoulder back into joint—look enticing, it was hardly surprising that we were drawn to his profession. Medicine might not have had as strong an appeal for Johnny as it did for me—among other possible reasons, he didn't share my ambition to forge a life different from the one I'd been born into in Willow Falls—but once we showed an interest, Dr. Dunbar seemed eager to share his knowledge and experience with us.

I couldn't be sure exactly when Johnny's medical education began, but I knew to the minute when mine did. I was eight years old, and I woke on a summer night to find Dr. Dunbar sitting on the edge of my bed. I knew who he was, but only vaguely. At that point Johnny and I were only friends as part of a larger group of same-aged boys, and I didn't associate him with the physician I'd seen for a school checkup. But that night Dr. Dunbar turned on the light beside my bed and softly spoke my name. "Matthew? Matt?" He patted my leg tenderly.

As soon as he thought I was fully awake, Dr. Dunbar said, "Matthew, your father is dead."

I barely had time to gasp before he went on. "He was killed in an automobile accident."

"What . . . what happened?"

"He ruptured his spleen." Dr. Dunbar was to be forgiven for this response. I'd wanted to know about the accident itself, but he'd answered according to how his profession interpreted curiosity. "Do you know where your spleen is?"

I shook my head. Dr. Dunbar reached over and pressed three fingers against my abdomen. He poked hard to impress me with that area's softness and vulnerability, and to make certain I understood what he was telling me.

"His spleen . . . ruptured?"

"The spleen's job," he explained, "is to filter out impurities in the blood. It's enclosed in a thin capsule, and when that capsule ruptures, blood rushes into the abdominal cavity. When that happens, no one can survive for long."

Then he subtly shifted from a physician's rough tour of anatomy to a family friend's gentle rub. "I'm sorry, Matthew. Your father thought the world of you. He was a good man. We'll all miss him." Did Dr. Dunbar know these things to be true of my father, or was he simply trying to help me feel better?

Dr. Dunbar's strategy for breaking the news about my father's death was unusual, but it worked as well as anything could. Detailing that fatal injury had the simultaneous—and paradoxical—effect of hitting me hard with the stark fact of his death and diffusing the force of that blow. With my stomach still tender from the pressure of the doctor's fingers, I had to concentrate on the physical reality of death, and that diverted me momentarily from thinking about what life would be like without my father. And then on some level I was also flattered that Dr. Dunbar believed I was mature and intelligent enough to handle the hard fact of death along with its complicated physiology.

Dr. Dunbar waited another moment to make sure of my composure, and then said, "Why don't you get up now. Your mother needs you."

With Dr. Dunbar's hand resting gently on my shoulder, we moved into the living room, where my mother sat quietly weeping. Her brother was there too, and as I walked into my mother's arms, in the instant before my own tears commenced, I looked over at my uncle and thought, *I know where the spleen is.*

Had Dr. Dunbar already seen something in me before that night, something that led him to conclude I had promise as a physician? And when I took the news of my father's death without wincing, did he realize that I might have the ability to perform a doctor's most difficult task—to look into someone's eyes and give them the hardest news they could ever get? Or had I impressed him with my question about the spleen, suggesting a curiosity that could not be quelled even in the darkest moment?

Whenever our "education" began, Johnny and I were well embarked on our unofficial course of study by the time we were teenagers. In fact, if patients consented, we were occasionally allowed to be present during a treatment or examination. When June Dunbar complained of an earache, for example, Dr. Dunbar let us look through the otoscope, and pointed out the swollen red membrane that indicated an ear infection. And he once summoned us to the clinic to witness him taking a swab of Betty Schaeffer's niece's throat, in order to determine if she had strep throat. Harold Schmitke gave us permission to watch while Dr. Dunbar put four stitches in Mr. Schmitke's forehead, repairing the damage done by a storm window that had slipped from his hands. We listened to many heartbeats and breaths both deep and shallow; we tapped knees with rubber hammers and attached blood-pressure cuffs; we took pulses and temperatures and watched blood be drawn; we looked at x-rays and learned to see broken bones and lungs with pneumonia. Most of Willow Falls came to refer to us as "Dr. Dunbar's boys," and regarded our medical ambitions with tolerance and amusement.

The vast majority of Dr. Dunbar's instruction came in conversation rather than in the presence of patients. "I saw something today," he might say, "that I haven't encountered in years." Then, the hook set, he'd tell us about a patient's bulging eyes, and how they tipped him off to a thyroid condition. Or, shaking his head, he would remark, "I was afraid that finger would have to come off," and go on to explain the circulatory problems a diabetic could face. And he once held up his hand for a long moment before describing exactly what that hand felt as he palpated an abdomen and felt the mass that led to the discovery of the tumor that killed Mr. Jensen.

But a bullet wound! Bullet wounds were the stuff of movies and television, and then Louisa Lindahl had not accidentally shot herself while cleaning a weapon—she was the victim of a crime! I couldn't help but think that we were about to be part of something glamorous and mysterious. And as we followed Dr. Dunbar toward his clinic, I considered the status I'd have at school, with my insider's knowledge of the event all of Willow Falls would be talking about.

As he opened the door to the clinic, the doctor said, "The deputy's search party found her stumbling along Highway K. Doubled over and bleeding and nearly frozen from being out in the cold in nothing but a thin dress. I wasn't sure whether it was more urgent to treat her for the gunshot wound or for frostbite."

The clinic consisted of a reception area and three small examination rooms, and Dr. Dunbar led us toward the only lighted room. Dr. Dunbar had turned up the heat to thaw out Miss Lindahl, and the corridor was dark and warm.

"Is the deputy here?" Johnny asked.

"He's back at the jail. Interrogating the assailant. He'll be back later if she's up to answering questions."

In the open doorway, I had my own moment of hesitation. The blood trail that we couldn't find in the woods was evident now, quarter- and nickel-sized drops dried to a dusty burgundy led to the examination table, where an unconscious woman lay beneath a bright lamp. She was covered with a sheet and a blanket, but her head, neck, and shoulders were bare.

For a moment, I wondered if Dr. Dunbar had invited us into the clinic not to give us a lesson about bullet wounds, but rather to teach us about death. The young woman's flesh was beyond pale. It was marmoreal, and I couldn't help but think that I was looking at a corpse. And then I recognized her. For while the name Louisa Lindahl was unknown to me, the face was not.

Burke's Pharmacy was a popular after-school spot in town, and this young woman worked at its soda fountain, scooping ice cream, mixing phosphates, pouring Cokes, and dodging the straw wrappers frequently blown her way. She wasn't much older than the teenage patrons, but she showed no interest in us except as customers.

She was tall, slender, and pretty in a way unfamiliar to most of us. She wore no makeup, but her luminous skin and excellent bone structure made the lipstick and eye shadow that the girls our age had begun to wear unnecessary. Her neck was long, and her jaw was delicate but square. Her chestnut hair was not tightly pin-curled or overly coiffed, but simply tied back or piled on top of her head without regard to style or fashion. She wore faded print dresses that looked as if they came out of a grandmother's closet, though these dresses must have been a smaller person's hand-me-downs, for they always looked a bit too tight, and the hems and sleeves too short. And yet along with an element of aloofness, her austere, gray-eyed loveliness gave her a refined, almost aristocratic appearance, at least to my small-town eyes. These contradictions fascinated me—not only the shabby attire coupled with her regal beauty, but also the good looks with no apparent attempt to adorn or enhance them. And then there was the fact that she was a waitress, but seemed completely indifferent to pleasing people. . . .

No matter how those of us boys sitting at the soda fountain teased or interrogated her (the girls pretended not to notice her), she wouldn't say much of anything beyond what her work required. And she always refused to disclose where she was from or why she had come to our town. She even resisted the entreaties and flirtations directed her way by more accomplished suitors. I was sitting at the counter one Friday afternoon, when Rick Carver took his best shot. Rick had graduated from Willow Falls High a few years before, and he was known for scoring both on and off the basketball court. Tall, blond, and possessed of an irresistible smile, Rick attended Augustana College on a scholarship, but he came home occasionally to mingle with mortals. On that day, however, he might as well have been a stammering high school freshman. After trying repeatedly to attract her interest, he finally resigned himself to failure, spun off his stool, softly cursed, and walked out of Burke's. She didn't even watch him go, and a part of me silently cheered.

But none of the previous impressions I had of Louisa Lindahl, none of the intriguing ambiguities or puzzling paradoxes, could possibly match the salient facts of this day: *Tarpaper shack. Lester Huston. Gunshot wound.*

Dr. Dunbar led the way into the room, and we arranged

ourselves at the examination table, the doctor on one side, Johnny and I on the other, and the unconscious Louisa Lindahl between us.

"This young lady," Dr. Dunbar said, "should be rechristened. A more appropriate name for her would be Lucky Lindahl. She was shot in the torso with a small-caliber pistol, probably a .22, and if you think that gun's smaller slug and slower velocity would constitute a reduced threat to her, you'd be sorely mistaken. At close range a .22 can do plenty of damage. But in this case her assailant could not have injured her any less severely if he had been trying. Look here—"

Slowly, as if his main concern was not to wake the patient, Dr. Dunbar pulled the blanket down to her knees. Only a sheet covered her now, and beneath it the contours of her naked body were apparent.

Dr. Dunbar next took hold of the top of the sheet, but then he left it in place. "Matt, there's another sheet in that cabinet behind you. Would you get it for me, please?"

I tugged open a drawer, and was greeted by the smell of bleached linens. I handed a folded sheet to the doctor, and he looked Louisa Lindahl up and down. "How shall we do this?"

He partially unfolded the sheet I gave him, and draped it across her upper body, right on top of the other sheet. Then he pulled the lower sheet down below her navel. For an instant, however, this maneuver left her breasts uncovered, an error he hastily corrected by pulling down the top sheet.

The glimpse I had of Louisa Lindahl's breasts can't have lasted much more than a second. But it was enough time to take in breasts perfect in their symmetry, pale and faintly blue-veined. The rose-colored aureoles were the size of silver dollars, and there was a tiny slit in each nipple. The breasts were large enough to sag slightly to the side from their own weight.

The doctor didn't acknowledge the accident with the sheets—no oops, no embarrassed laugh, no humorous remark. In fact, he whisked that sheet back in place so swiftly, so dexterously, that I wondered if he had been testing us, the way he did when he asked us if a boy who cut his foot on a brick at a construction site should be given a tetanus shot. Perhaps he wanted to know if we were mature enough, if we were serious enough about the profession we said we were interested in, to be shown a young woman's breasts without making a wisecrack to conceal our titillation or discomfort?

If we were being tested, Johnny might have received a lower score. He gasped when Louisa Lindahl's breasts were first revealed, though it wasn't much as gasps go, just a quick intake of breath, closer to a pain-induced wince than it was to any sound associated with pleasure. I'm not even sure his father heard it. A look might have passed between them, but I couldn't be certain. I was unpracticed in the subtle communications between fathers and sons.

A bullet wound was uncommon in Willow Falls, of course, but I had already learned from being around Dr. Dunbar that doctors—and, for that matter, those interested in becoming doctors—differ from other people in a fundamental way: they generally want to get closer to the sights that most people want to turn away from. And when Dr. Dunbar directed us to the wound traversing Louisa Lindahl's midsection—a foot-wide gash sewn shut with fourteen sutures and painted amber with betadine—the eyes closest to her torso were the doctor's and mine.

"Do you see why I call her lucky?" Dr. Dunbar said, tracing the wound in the air just inches above her abdomen. "Her assailant was plainly trying to end her life. He wasn't aiming at an arm or a leg. She probably turned to the side just when he fired at her, and the bullet tunneled under a couple layers of skin and then from one side of her to the other. An inch or two deeper in and who knows what kind of damage it might have done."

"But an inch the other way and it would have missed her completely," said Johnny.

Even without the benefit of Dr. Dunbar's peeved look, I knew that Johnny's suggestion was not consistent with the lessons his father was trying to teach. "If the bullet had gone in an inch deeper," I asked, "wouldn't it have passed through her liver?"

He cocked his head as if he needed that alteration of perspective to note the arrangement of her organs. "Liver? Maybe so. . . . It could have even hit a rib, and when a projectile hits bone, you generally have serious trouble. Then you can get fragments—of bullet or bone—flying off in any direction."

Dr. Dunbar stepped back from Louisa Lindahl, and while Johnny must have understood that we were to do the same, I missed the message. I remained bent over the wound, my face less than a foot from Louisa Lindahl's flesh. I could smell the antiseptic, and under that, faintly, something else. . . . Blood perhaps, maybe nicotine, and then something deeper, muskier, a smell belonging to Louisa Lindahl's essence. The black knots of the sutures looked like flies lined up along her pale abdomen. I had to touch her—how could I come this close and not?—and yet I couldn't decide where. I paused, my hand hovering over her.

That hesitation provided enough time for the doctor to speak my name—"Matthew!"—and step toward me.

But by then it was too late. I placed my palm lightly on Louisa Lindahl's belly, just below the furrow of flesh that Dr. Dunbar's stitches had closed. The tip of my little finger slipped into her navel with such ease it seemed to have found its natural place.

My hand rested there for no longer than Louisa Lindahl's breasts had been bared, but it was long enough for the feeling of her cool soft skin to stamp itself into my memory indelibly.

I jerked my hand back and stood up just in time to escape Dr. Dunbar's attempt to swat me away.

"Matthew! What the hell do you think you're doing?"

"I just wanted to see if she felt . . . cold."

"You never touch, Matthew. Not without the patient's permission. I invited you in here because it's a unique learning situation. It's not an opportunity for you to indulge your personal curiosity."

"Sorry."

He stared sternly at me for a long moment. "Did I make a mistake inviting you in here?" To make clear that the question was meant for both of us, he shifted his gaze to Johnny and then back to me.

"No sir," I said, intending to answer for both of us.

"You're still interested in learning something?"

I nodded eagerly.

"Johnny?"

"Sure."

Once he was assured that he had our attention again, Dr. Dunbar proceeded to lecture us on primary and secondary wounds, temporary and permanent cavities, and the stretching and displacement of tissue. Dr. Dunbar got no closer to combat than a New Jersey Army hospital during the Second World War, and I couldn't help but wonder if this part of the lesson was intended not only to educate us, but to impress us with his knowledge of ballistics.

And knowing what we had seen of Miss Lindahl, perhaps he wanted to stress the clinical nature of the situation as well. After all, the girl lying there before us was not to be looked at for her naked beauty, but rather as a patient in need of a physician's help. She was her wound, and the purpose of Dr. Dunbar's lecture was to remind us of that.

But I couldn't help myself. I wanted to know so much more than debridement techniques and the dangers of sepsis. "Why'd you knock her out?" I asked.

Dr. Dunbar's reply came in tones as icy as his earlier glare. "Knock her out? I didn't knock her out. I anesthetized her. When she came in she was in pain, in shock, and bleeding. I wasn't sure of the extent of her injuries, or what she'd require in the way of treatment."

The tension that had developed in the room seemed to make Johnny uneasy, and he rushed to ask an easily answered question: "So there's no chance she will die?"

"She will not die."

"Will she have a bad scar?"

"A bad scar? Depends on what you mean by bad. You saw how her body is already trying to heal itself. The scar will be the mark of how well it succeeds. I'd expect there to be some delling. You know what that is, don't you? It's a little depression, like a dimple. And then sometimes the body does too good a job, so to speak. She could develop a keloid, a scar that doesn't know when to stop. I know you've seen those—the flesh mounds up, the skin acquires a sheen. Depending on its size it might even look pulpy. . . ."

Louisa Lindahl stirred beneath the sheet, her body twitching and rippling as if an electric current were coursing through it. Dr. Dunbar was suddenly alert, watching for a sign that would probably be meaningless or invisible to Johnny or me. He stepped forward and placed his hand on her shoulder, his fingers extending just below her clavicle, where neither organ nor vital sign pulsed. Instantly, as if his touch had thrown a switch, her contractions ceased.

"How did you do that?" I asked.

The doctor merely smiled. It was the same smile he'd worn when he sent us on our way with pockets full of gauze.

## 4.

WHEN I ARRIVED HOME THAT NIGHT my mother was in
her customary place and engaged in her favorite activity.
The telephone cord stretched from the wall to the kitchen
table, where she sat with the black receiver in one hand
and a Pall Mall in the other. She was wearing a bathrobe,
her usual after-work attire, and her hair was done up in
curlers. The room's only light came from the fluorescent
strip along the back of the stove. In contrast to the Dunbar
home, where the aroma of Mrs. Dunbar's turkey and all the
sumptuous extras still hung in the air, our house smelled
like cabbage, though my mother hadn't prepared cabbage
in weeks.

Whoever was on the other end of the line was telling
my mother something so fascinating that she couldn't be
bothered to greet me. Nevertheless, she held up her hand
to indicate that I was to wait in the room until her conversation was finished.

My mother loved gossip, though she never would have
called it that. She'd lived in Willow Falls all her life, and for
her staying abreast of its citizens and their activities was
like keeping up with the family. And between her job and

her network of female friends, she had access to plenty of information, as well as the means to move it along. This proclivity of hers didn't bother me much. She put in long hours on her feet at work and then came home to cook, clean, and pinch pennies. I understood that she took her pleasures where she could. Besides, I often picked up a few juicy rumors about our town's mostly respectable citizens, some of them parents of my schoolmates.

She said good-bye and handed the receiver to me so I could walk it back to the cradle.

"Sadie?" I asked. It was a good bet. My mother usually concluded her day talking with Sadie Pruitt, even if the two of them had just worked the evening shift together at Palmer's.

"Doris Greiner."

"What did Doris have to say?"

"Mrs. Greiner," my mother corrected. "She said a young woman got herself shot today. But you'd know all about that, wouldn't you?"

"They brought her to Dr. Dunbar."

"Saved her life, did he?"

"I don't know about that, but she's going to live."

She nodded and crossed her legs in order to massage an aching foot. But she'd be back on her feet at Palmer's the following day. The hair curlers told me that. My mother was a homely woman, but she tried to look her best at work. She'd wear a little rouge to add color to her sallow cheeks, and lipstick to help define her narrow mouth's tight line. Mascara and eyeliner would make her eyes seem less small and close-set. The curlers would put a little wave in her steel-gray hair. Nothing could make her figure anything but stick-thin—smoking and long hours on her feet saw to that—but her uniform would be clean and pressed, her shoes polished. In the end, however, the good tips my mother usually received came because she worked hard to see to her customers' needs, not because she charmed them. And she wouldn't have had it any other way.

"I take it the gunshot wound wasn't serious then?"

My mother was seeking corroboration for what she had heard from Doris Greiner, that and the small odd, possibly lurid detail that her regular informants might not have provided.

"A superficial abdominal laceration," I said, not entirely sure of the rightness of the terminology, but proud nevertheless of my ability to use it.

"Lucky gal."

"That's what the doctor said."

"You know anything else about her?"

"She worked at Burke's. Lindahl. Louisa Lindahl. But you already know that."

She blew a stream of smoke toward the ceiling. "She was living with the fellow who shot her. Lester Huston. Not married to, living with." My mother was no moralist, but she obviously regarded this piece of information as essential to the narrative. "You know anything about him?"

"Not a thing."

"Except that he had a bad temper."

That verb's tense almost slipped by me. "Had?"

Before answering, she devoted an unusual amount of time and care to pinching a scrap of tobacco from her lip. Then, as if she'd decided the entire smoking enterprise wasn't worth the bother, she crushed out the cigarette.

She looked up at me, vaguely surprised. "You didn't hear? Lester Huston killed himself in the county jail. Tore up a sheet, tied one end around his neck and the other around the frame of his cot, and then just leaned forward and strangled himself."

"Damn!"

"So, no trial for Mr. Huston. And no getting up on the witness stand for Miss Lindahl."

"Jesus Christ. He strangled himself?"

"Doris says that's why they don't have lights or any overhead fixtures in the cells. So the prisoners can't hang themselves. But I guess where there's a will there's a way."

"Nobody at the Dunbars' said anything about . . ."

"Maybe they don't know. This is fresh news." She stood and straightened her robe. "I guess your doctor can't save 'em all."

That remark's nasty edge was almost surely not an accident. I'd always suspected that my mother didn't like Dr. Dunbar, and while jealousy would have been the obvious explanation, I doubted that was it. She knew I looked up to the doctor, and that I'd attached myself to the family. But those things didn't seem to bother her. She subscribed to the laissez-faire school of parenting, a philosophy that reflected her own upbringing. She was the seventh of eleven children, and growing up on a dusty little family farm during the Depression fostered in her the belief that we all had to look out for ourselves in this world. Accordingly, she felt she was fulfilling her parental duties by providing food and shelter for her only child. As long as I stayed in school and out of jail, she'd stay out of my life.

No, my mother's dislike of the doctor didn't have its source in jealousy, not least because she believed it was a sin to be impressed by another human being. Her feelings about Rex Dunbar could best be understood in the context of the town's divided opinion of itself. On one side were the town's civic leaders and politicians, its merchants and professionals, and the wives of those men. Those people genuinely believed in the town's slogan—"a city on the rise"—though the use of the term "city" was a bit overstated in light of the fact that its population was right around two thousand at the time. They truly thought that more people hadn't settled in Willow Falls only because they didn't know about it. And they saw the presence of Dr. Dunbar as corroboration of their view of Willow Falls as a special place. After all, the Dunbars were discerning, intelligent people, and they could only have chosen Willow Falls because they could see the town for what it was—a desirable place to make a life and raise a family. The attractive and refined Dr. and Mrs. Dunbar, in turn, gave the town a glitter it never had before they arrived. If Willow Falls could see the image of Rex Dunbar when it looked into the mirror, life there had to be ascendant.

My mother was squarely in the other camp, which included all those suspicious of outsiders and uneasy at the prospect of change. They felt that the Dunbars' fine clothes, their grand house, and their trips to Minneapolis to take in the symphony or ballet were not markers of culture and sophistication, but rather of ostentation. And for many Minnesotans, there could be no greater failing. These folks were determinedly unpretentious, and their sense that life in Willow Falls didn't amount to much was consistent with their perspective on life in general. In our wind-blown part of the world, where nothing rose higher than a few cottonwoods, to want too much or to reach too high was to set yourself up for inevitable disappointment. Not surprisingly, most of the people who felt this way had farming in their background; they might have been town dwellers by this point, but not for more than a generation or two, and they likely had a relative or two who still lived out in the country.

Before leaving the kitchen, my mother said, "Phil asked if you want to bus tables during your Christmas vacation. He's willing to hire you on."

Phil Palmer was my mother's employer, and I knew she would have asked him for this favor. "I'm thinking about it."

"Don't think too long."

My mother walked out of the kitchen, but then returned almost immediately to retrieve her Pall Malls. And she had another question for me. "How does Mrs. Dunbar fix her stuffing?"

"She mixes in sausage. And slices of apple. To keep it moist, she says."

"Sausage and apple . . . huh!" Her eyebrows rose as if she found Mrs. Dunbar's method of preparing dressing more baffling than the news of the shooting.

"It was good."

"I'll take your word for it. Have you had your fill of turkey yet? If you haven't, I could make a little one for us. But big enough so we'd have some extra for sandwiches."

"That's okay."

"Well, let me know if you change your mind. Red Owl's going to sell their leftover birds cheap."

"But it wouldn't be for Thanksgiving."

"No, but it'd be turkey."

I knew the Dunbar house so well that I could tell which of their four telephones Mrs. Dunbar had answered from the sound of her footsteps as she walked away to find her son after putting the receiver down. High heels on the wood floors—the telephone on the small table next to the wide staircase.

As soon as Johnny came on the line I asked, "Did you hear about Lester Huston?"

"Yeah," he replied. "Deputy Greiner called a little while ago to tell Dad what happened. Dad lit into him because apparently Greiner told Lester Huston that Louisa Lindahl was in critical condition. He made it sound like she was going to die. So Lester Huston thought there was a good chance he'd be charged with murder."

"What the hell did Greiner do that for?"

"That's what Dad asked him. The deputy kept saying it was part of his interrogation. Dad told him that when Sheriff Hart gets back to town he's going to hear what a screwup he has for a deputy."

"Man, what I would've given to hear your dad read Greiner the riot act!"

"He was pissed, all right. Royally pissed."

Before that day I would have had a hard time imagining Dr. Dunbar angry. But now I had seen his expression when I touched Louisa Lindahl's stomach.

"Does Louisa Lindahl know Huston's dead?"

"Dad went upstairs to break the news to her a few minutes ago."

"Upstairs?"

"Dad didn't want her spending the night in the clinic. There aren't any real beds in there, and it would have been too far away if she needed something during the night. So we moved her upstairs to that little back bedroom."

"It was okay to move her? Jesus, she was shot—. And you helped? Did you carry her or what?"

"She could walk a little, but only a couple steps. We tried propping her up between us, but she couldn't raise her arms to put them around our shoulders because it pulled too hard on her stitches. So finally Dad just carried her."

"He carried her? Up the stairs?"

Johnny laughed. "Sure, he's a doctor!"

"Did she say anything, you know, when you were trying to help her?"

"Nah. She barely knew where she was. But when we helped her off the table, she whispered, 'Fuck.'"

Lying awake in bed that night, I tried in vain to recall the sight of Louisa Lindahl's breasts. But try as I might I couldn't concentrate on that image. Instead, questions kept imposing themselves. What, I wondered, would make a man lean into his own death when all he needed to do to save his life was sit back and slacken the noose that he himself had knotted? Was it fear of the punishment he'd receive, or did he find unbearable the realization that he had killed the woman he'd loved?

## 5

AMONG DR. DUNBAR'S MANY CONTRIBUTIONS to civic life in Willow Falls—serving on the school board, standing by as physician-in-attendance at high school athletic events, heading up charity drives—he organized hockey in our town.

Though we clearly did have a climate conducive to the sport—our ponds and the Willow River usually had at least a skin of ice by Thanksgiving—hockey was not popular in our part of the state. In northern Minnesota boys laced up their skates and grabbed a stick as soon as they could walk, but in Willow Falls the big sports were baseball, football, and basketball, as well as hunting and fishing. Dummett's Hardware sold pucks, sticks, and skates, but there were no school or amateur hockey programs, and no public ice was maintained for the sport. A few kids whacked a puck around on one of the public rinks from time to time, but until Dr. Dunbar came to town there were never hockey games. He had played hockey in high school and college, he loved the sport, and he wasn't about to give it up just because the residents of our town had wobbly ankles and didn't know a hip check from a glove save.

Every year then, once the cold weather came to stay, Dr. Dunbar converted a carefully measured section of their big backyard into a skating rink. And while the children in Willow Falls were welcome to use the rink to practice figure eights or to play crack-the-whip during the week, on weekends the ice was reserved for hockey games. You had to be at least high school age to play, and over the years a few men became passable players—usually enough, anyway, for two full teams.

When Johnny and I were growing up, Dr. Dunbar provided us with plenty of instruction on the ice. But until we came of age, we stood along the sidelines with the rest of the spectators—at least fifty people would often show up to watch the weekend games. Even when there was little chance we'd be invited to play, though, we always came prepared. We wore our skates, our supporters and cups (we called them "cans"), and we wrapped newspapers or magazines around our shins. Finally, when we were sixteen, we were allowed to take part in the competition.

In truth, however, those pickup games were far more recreational than they were competitive. What would have landed a player in the penalty box in a real hockey game was likely to be accidental and followed by an apology on our rink. Body checks were more like the suggestion of what an actual check might be, and there was never an occasion when players were tempted to throw down their gloves and square off. And Dr. Dunbar and the Burrows brothers, Stan and Don, were the only players who wore hockey gloves or pads. More often than not, Dr. Dunbar also wore his old Wolverines jersey. The rest of us were out there in wool mackinaws, sweatshirts, and mittens. No one wore a helmet or a mask, but back then very few professional players did either.

The Burrows brothers were pretty fair hockey players. They'd grown up in Grand Forks, North Dakota, and played in high school. Red Rayner was from Warroad, Minnesota, and he could play, too. A few more men had some hockey in their past, and still others developed a few skills just from playing over the years, but Dr. Dunbar was indisputably the best player. Born and raised in northern Michigan, he attended the University of Michigan on a hockey scholarship, and though he had an opportunity to play junior-league hockey after graduation, by then he had decided on a career in medicine.

Every time he laced up his skates, though, his talent and skill returned, and his superiority to every other player was apparent. He skated backward faster than most of us could move forward, and he handled the puck as dexterously as the rest of us might flip a coin and pass it from hand to hand. On the ice he had agility and grace that would have been astonishing if you only saw him sitting behind his desk in a suit. And if you were lucky enough to be on his team, your game improved instantly. He'd pass the puck to you in such a way that it didn't even seem as if you had to catch it; it would simply land on your stick at exactly the instant when it had to be there. And with what seemed to be little more than a flick of the wrist, his shots on goal flew from his stick as if the puck were rocket propelled.

One Sunday a few weeks after that Thanksgiving Day when Louisa Lindahl was brought to the doctor's clinic, we gathered for a game. There was no wind at all, and snow was falling at a rate of over an inch an hour, covering the drifts that had been on the ground since Thanksgiving. The flakes fell straight down like a heavy veil, but Dr. Dunbar was not to be deterred. He and a few other men brought out snow shovels, cleared the ice, and the game was on. A few wives, girlfriends, younger brothers and sisters were on hand as spectators, the snow gathering on their coats and hats faster than they could brush it away. They clapped as much to keep warm as to cheer us on. And Janet and Julia skipped from one side of the ice to the other, shouting encouragement to their father, Johnny, or me, their allegiance dictated by who was closest to the puck.

Johnny and his father played on the same team that afternoon, with the Burrows brothers on the opposite team for the sake of competitive balance. I was on the Burrows' team, but I didn't contribute much. My hockey skills were limited to getting up and down the ice in a hurry, so long as I could travel in a straight line.

Our games usually started slowly, as we all adjusted to being on skates and the older players allowed their joints to thaw. That day the heavy snow made all of us even more tentative in our first few trips up and down the ice. Soon, however, we were at full speed, though the pace varied considerably from player to player, and it was interrupted frequently that afternoon in any case, in order to clear the ice of snow.

Shortly after one of those breaks, Johnny was skating up the side of the rink with the puck. I had a clear shot at him, and when I hit him with a shoulder check, he flew off the ice and into a snow pile with a thump. The hit was legal, but the collision was more violent than I expected it to be, perhaps because I caught Johnny completely by surprise, the contact coming before he could do a thing to prepare himself.

But other than having the wind knocked out of him and getting some snow down his collar, Johnny was unhurt, and he waved off my apology. Back on the ice, he skated alongside me, and said with a smile, "I hope that's just a phase you're going through."

It was a private joke. In sixth grade our teacher had been the soft-hearted Miss Dell, and she never scolded her students with anything stronger than that phrase. Johnny and I adopted it as our slogan, and any punch in the arm, failed joke, or clumsy mistake would likely provide an occasion for one of us to recite Miss Dell's words.

After I slammed into Johnny, however, something in the game changed. Only a couple minutes later, the doctor and I tangled behind the goal—chicken wire stretched between two steel pipes—and while we were scrambling for the puck, he jabbed me hard in the ribs with the butt end of his stick. Only a few minutes later, he hip-checked me so hard he knocked me off my skates. I landed hard and slid into the knees of another player who almost fell on top of me.

I had no doubt that the doctor was singling me out for this treatment, and though it made me mad, there was nothing I could do to get back at him. If I tried to skate into him, he'd spin away and make me miss, perhaps with another check to hurry me on my way.

But anger and adrenaline now fueled my game, and I soon intercepted a pass and broke away with a clear path to the goal. Bent low and moving fast down the center of the rink with the puck out in front of me, I had only the goalie to contend with, the wide-bodied but slow-handed Dennis McMaster.

Then something rapped my ankle. At first I thought I had kicked myself with my own skate as I sprinted down the ice. Another bump came, and this time I knew I hadn't done it to myself. Then, before I knew exactly what had happened, I was off my skates and sliding along on my chest, the puck wobbling ineffectually out in front of me and my stick trailing off in another direction.

I could do nothing to control the direction or speed of my slide, and I realized too late that I was heading for one of the pipes. My mittened hand and wrist kept my head from taking the full force of the impact, but the blow came hard enough. And just as it did, it occurred to me that it was Dr. Dunbar who had tripped me up.

The doctor skated up quickly, joining Dennis McMaster beside the goal. "You okay, Matt?" Dennis asked.

"Yeah." The answer was reflexive. I hadn't had time yet to access my injuries.

I tried to pull myself to my feet, using for support the same pipe I'd banged into. A skate slid out from under me, but before I fell again Johnny was there, his arm under my armpit, steadying and lifting me.

"Doesn't count," he said with a smile, "if your head goes into the net. It's got to be the puck."

"Head. Puck. I get those mixed up." I tasted blood, and began to probe carefully with my tongue to determine if I'd lost any teeth. They were all there, but blood filled my mouth and I spit, streaking the snow.

My cheek. I had bit my cheek.

"Goddamn, Matt," Dennis said, a comment I initially thought was prompted by my bloody expectoration.

Dr. Dunbar dropped his stick, thrust his hand under his arm to pull off his glove, and reached toward me. "Better let me look at that, Matthew."

I assumed he was referring to the hole in my cheek, but when I opened my mouth and tilted my head a curtain of red fell over one eye.

Either the ice or the steel pipe had opened a gash over my eye, and that was the injury that concerned Dr. Dunbar. I tried to wipe away the blood, but a red fog immediately clouded my vision.

Dr. Dunbar gently pushed my hand out of the way and inspected my injury. His fingers were warm on my forehead. After gently prodding the split skin around my eyebrow, he said, "Let's go inside, Matthew. We need to take care of that cut."

As the doctor and I walked off the ice, he made no apologies for having played a part in my fall. But I knew instinctively what he'd done. I'd underestimated how protective he felt toward Johnny, and how far a father would be willing to go in order to seek retribution for an injury to his son.

The people standing around the rink parted to allow the doctor and me to pass. The twins hurried over to check out my injury. Julia turned away at the sight of my blood, while Janet tried to get closer and said, "Ooh, Matt, your eye!"

"He'll be all right," said the doctor. "We'll just take him inside and put a Band-Aid on it."

It seemed clear that he was minimizing my injury for

the sake of his daughters' peace of mind, but the doctor's words still calmed me.

Dr. Dunbar and I stopped on the porch to take off our skates. He removed his first, then squatted down to unlace mine, enabling me to tilt my head back and keep the heel of my hand pressed to my eye.

"You wait here, Matt," Dr. Dunbar said. "I'll go find a towel or something so we can walk through the house without you bleeding on Mrs. Dunbar's carpet. And if you feel thirsty, help yourself." He pointed to a galvanized washtub packed with snow and bottles of Miller High Life and Coca Cola, the after-hockey refreshments he always provided. "But even if you don't want anything to drink," he added, "grab a handful of snow and hold it over your eye. It'll slow the bleeding."

I could hear the familiar sounds of the game behind me—the *clack clack* of wooden sticks colliding, and the *skrrk skrrk* of sharpened steel on ice. Would I ever hear those again without remembering the taste of blood? I shivered as my sweat cooled beneath the layers of clothes.

Just as Dr. Dunbar reached for the door, it opened from the inside, and I inhaled sharply when I saw who was standing there. "I was watching," said Louisa Lindahl. "I saw what happened." She held out a rag she'd brought for my wound.

Not long after the doctor stitched her up that fateful Thanksgiving Day, Louisa Lindahl was back on her feet, though they didn't take her far. Once it became apparent that the young woman had no resources and no place to go, the Dunbars told her she could move in with them.

She could work in the clinic, handling some of the clerical work, thereby freeing Betty Schaeffer to concentrate on nursing. Louisa accepted the offer, and she had been helping Mrs. Dunbar with household chores as well as working in the clinic. She was staying in the back bedroom upstairs, the same one Dr. Dunbar had carried her to after treating her for the bullet wound.

But I knew all this already, and so I was not surprised to see her. No, my sharp intake of breath was caused by something else.

Since that day when I'd stood over her in the clinic, I'd been completely taken with Louisa Lindahl. It was too soon to call it love and too simple to call it lust, but I felt something powerful, and whatever it was would have had me following her from room to wainscoted room in the Dunbar house if I could have done so without attracting the wrong kind of attention. She, on the other hand, had given no sign of noticing me. Except once.

A week earlier Louisa was alone in the kitchen, putting away dishes, when I came in looking for glue for a science project Johnny and I were working on upstairs. I generally had no trouble making conversation with girls who interested me, but I lost all courage in Louisa Lindahl's presence. Her haughty beauty was as intimidating as it was alluring, and she was in her twenties. And then there was the fact that I'd seen her unconscious and unclothed, a delicious secret knowledge that nonetheless put an even tighter clamp on my mouth. Finally, there was that matter of the gunshot wound. I had no idea how that factored into the whole equation, but it could hardly be ignored.

I said hello that night, but received no greeting in

return, which was exactly what usually happened when our paths crossed in the presence of others in the Dunbar home. Then, as I was on my way out of the room with the bottle of Elmer's, Louisa Lindahl said, "Nice of the Dunbars to take in strays and give them the run of the place, eh?"

I'm not sure what kept me from arguing with her, in spite of the fact that that was my first impulse. Was it the fear that this was an argument I would lose? Or could it possibly be the notion that I might benefit in the future from her belief that she and I had something in common? Whatever the reason, I stammered, "I guess," and hurried from the room.

Now, when Dr. Dunbar took the cloth that Louisa offered, a look passed between them. Even if my vision had not been restricted, I still wouldn't have been able to interpret it. Then the doctor smiled his best Rex Dunbar smile and said, "Anticipating my every need. Thank you, Louisa."

She returned his smile.

Dr. Dunbar folded the cloth into a rectangle the size of a paperback. "Press this over your eye, Matt." Behind me I heard a puck hit the pipe.

With his hand on my elbow, the doctor steered me inside. Mrs. Dunbar was in the kitchen, taking a tray of sugar cookies out of the oven. When she saw me and the bloody cloth, she exclaimed, "Oh my God, Matty!" Her expression of concern was that of a mother's.

"Take it easy, Alice. It looks worse than it is. A few stitches and Gordie Howe here will be right back out on the ice."

The doctor continued to guide me through the house

as if blood had blinded me in both eyes, and I could hear Louisa's footsteps as she followed close behind. She'd been watching the game . . . she'd seen what happened . . . but did she know why?

At the door to the clinic, Louisa asked, "Should I come in with you? Do you need any help?"

"No need," replied the doctor, much to my disappointment. "Matthew could probably sew himself up."

We went into the same examination room where Dr. Dunbar had treated Louisa Lindahl. "Lie down on the table, Matthew."

I did as I was told. I wasn't about to ask for it, but I wished I had the blanket he'd used to cover Louisa. My feet were freezing after standing out on the porch in my socks.

"Now, ordinarily I'd put a drape over the patient's face, leaving only the laceration exposed. Hell, you might like to watch. I have a hand mirror here in the drawer.

"All right."

Once I had the mirror in hand, I slowly took the compress away. Blood was leaking more than flowing from the cut, and that soon stopped when Dr. Dunbar numbed the area with lidocaine and epinephrine. "This is what a cut man uses to stop a boxer's bleeding." Dr. Dunbar was close enough that I could smell his sweat and his aftershave.

He continued to talk his way through the procedure, exactly as he would have done if I were watching him work on someone else. He cleaned the wound with 300 cc of saline solution and then prepared to sew. He explained the type of thread (6-0 nylon) and sutures (simple interrupted) he'd be using. "And notice that I'm not shaving your eyebrow, Matthew. Some doctors might do that, but it's not necessary. And I'd probably mar your good looks. Takes a hell of a long time for eyebrows to grow back. Different kind of hair."

I felt nothing but a vague tugging as the needle went in and out, and I watched my reflection with one eye while the doctor administered to the other, adding to the sense that I was more observer than patient.

He treated me so gently that I wondered again if I could have been wrong about what happened during the hockey game. Touch that tender didn't seem as if it could belong to the same man who had speared and then tripped me, sending me sprawling on the ice.

I handed the mirror back to him when he finished, but Dr. Dunbar wasn't through looking. He circled the table slowly, examining his handiwork from different angles.

"Any other injuries that need attending to?" he asked.

"I bit my cheek, but I think the bleeding's stopped."

Nevertheless, he inspected the inside of my mouth with the aid of a light and a tongue depressor. After a moment of probing he declared, "Nothing serious." He patted my shoulder. "You can sit up now."

I did, slowly.

"Feeling woozy?"

"A little."

"Take your time. Lie back down if you like."

"I'm okay."

"Sit for a minute. You're done playing for the day. This isn't the Stanley Cup."

I took a few deep breaths to steady myself, and the doctor

reached into a drawer to pull out a pack of Chesterfields. He sat down on a rolling stool and lit up, using a kidney-shaped steel bowl for an ashtray. Then, after taking another look at me, he held the bowl out toward me. "You need this? You think you might throw up?"

I hadn't cursed, cried, complained, or recoiled at any time during the procedure. I couldn't think of any other way to convince him that I could handle this except to say again, "I'm okay."

"You look pale." The doctor's tone puzzled me. It was oddly formal, almost grave, and not at all like the jocular, light-hearted Dr. Dunbar I knew. Was he angry with me? Did all this have to do with my having knocked Johnny off his skates?

"I feel fine." I considered insisting on lacing my skates back up and returning to the game.

"If you say so." He cocked his head as he looked at me. "You'll have a black eye."

"That's okay."

"Sure. It'll make you look like a tough guy. You want people to think you're a tough guy?"

So, it was about Johnny. "I never thought about it."

"Some girls go for that."

"I wouldn't know."

"Trust me."

He inhaled deeply on his cigarette. He made an incongruous sight, wearing his hockey jersey yet holding his cigarette in that elegant way he had. "You know, Matthew, there's more to hockey than just banging into people. You need skills to go along with your aggression. We used to have an expression that applied to guys like you. 'Getting ahead of your skates.' That's you out on the ice, Matt. Ahead of your skates."

I was right. Dr. Dunbar had wanted to teach me a lesson for hitting his son.

"I know I stink out there," I said. "So I try to hustle and skate hard and hope that makes up for it."

He ignored my comment. "I wonder if that's you in life, Matthew. Out ahead of your skates."

I understood that we were in the realm of metaphor, but I didn't really understand what was being said about my character. Still, I no more would have inquired after his meaning than I would have asked for a blanket to cover my cold feet.

"Maybe so." I got off the table.

Later that night, after my mother had gone to bed, I went into our little bathroom. I stood at the sink, in front of the faucet that always seemed to drip. Above it, the mirror's silver backing made every image seem as if it were decomposing before your very eyes. Under the harsh light, I undressed and inspected the injuries that the masculine code had prevented me from paying attention to earlier. The rectangular bruise on my side could not have been a more perfect impression of the butt of Dr. Dunbar's stick. The inside of my cheek was red, raw, and puckered. My eye was starting to blacken, the socket rimmed in deep purple. And the newly repaired cut throbbed as if my blood was trying to break free of the doctor's stitches.

## 6.

JOHNNY AND I HAD BEEN LOOKING FORWARD to Buzz Mallen's New Year's party for weeks. Buzz's parents would be in Saint Paul for the night, and his older brother had agreed to buy beer and hard liquor for the occasion. Then, only two days before the party, its format changed. Now it was going to be a small affair, one you could only gain entry to with a date. I had recently broken up with Debbie McCarren, my girlfriend of five months, because she felt we were "getting too serious," which was almost surely a euphemism for either "I want to date someone else," or "I'm tired of slapping away your roving hands." And since neither Johnny nor I could possibly find dates on such short notice, we resigned ourselves to missing the party.

Rather than give up completely on the idea of celebration, however, we improvised our own feeble party plan. Johnny's parents always went out on New Year's Eve, first to dinner at Palmer's (where I might have cleared their table had I not arranged to have the night off), and then to a dance at the Heritage House Hotel. The twins were sleeping over at the home of a friend. Johnny and I would have the Dunbar house more or less to ourselves. Along, I hoped, with Louisa Lindahl.

And so that New Year's Eve, Johnny and I lugged his record player up to the attic, along with a bag of potato chips, a log of summer sausage, a few cigars, two cans of Pabst Blue Ribbon, and a fifth of blackberry brandy I'd stolen from Palmer's. The large dusty space smelled of mold and unfinished wood from the heavy dark timbers slanting overhead. And because that night was exceptionally cold, we plugged in a space heater; its glowing bars and an old floor lamp illuminated the corner where we would usher in 1963. The attic was a deliberate choice. We'd both been drunk a few times, but that night we planned to reach a new level of inebriation, one that would require sequestration. We even designated a tin wastebasket as the receptacle if either of us had to throw up and couldn't make it down to the bathroom in time.

I loved the Dunbars' attic in part because my mother was ruthless about throwing out or giving away anything that wasn't essential to our lives. What other families saved for future generations or emergencies, or simply because they couldn't bear to throw it away, my mother banished as "junk." So when I entered the Dunbar attic, I felt as if I were in a place where time meant something more than the present moment, and items were saved for reasons other than mere utility. The Dunbar attic contained the usual assortment of old clothes and outgrown toys, broken furniture and holiday decorations, but all of it seemed to me part of an effort to perpetuate and preserve a family and its traditions. To me, it was as much museum as storage area.

We listened to our favorite album—the soundtrack to

*West Side Story*—over and over that evening. We'd seen the movie the previous summer, on a trip to Minneapolis with Mrs. Dunbar. (While the doctor tried to provide us with a medical education, Mrs. Dunbar tried to encourage our appreciation of culture.) It was the musical's sadder songs that best matched our mood that New Year's Eve. For while we tried to convince ourselves that the big party didn't interest us—after all, we were above the immature antics of our adolescent peers—we both knew we really wanted to be at Buzz Mallen's place.

We finished off the sausage and chips and washed them down with the beer. And we had just cracked the seal on the brandy and lit our cigars when I made the suggestion I'd had in mind all along.

"Hey," I said, trying to sound as if the idea had just occurred to me, "why don't you go find Louisa and see if she wants to join us?"

Johnny was sitting in an old armchair whose upholstery had torn and begun to leak stuffing, and I was in a rocker whose cane back had begun to unravel. "Louisa?" he said.

"You know—she lives in your house?"

"I thought this was going to be a stag night."

"She has to hear us up here. And she's sitting down there all alone on New Year's Eve. It's kind of rude, don't you think? Go ahead. If she doesn't want to, she'll just say no."

He puffed on his cigar and stared at me for a long moment. "Fine," he said. "If that's what you want."

While Johnny was gone, I looked around for another chair. I finally found a small metal folding chair, once part of a play set the twins had only recently outgrown. I sat down to try it, and then, confident the chair would support one of us if necessary, brought it over and put it under the lamp. I was using it as a footrest when Johnny reentered the attic.

He came toward me with an expression so glum I was certain he had failed to persuade Louisa to join us.

Then Johnny said, "We're over here," and I looked past him to Louisa Lindahl, who was just ascending the final step.

She paused for a moment to adjust to the dim light. "Is this where the party is?"

"Over here," Johnny said again.

As if she couldn't be sure of the safety of the planks beneath her feet, Louisa walked slowly toward us. When she stepped into our little circle of light, she took a long moment to gaze down at the arrangement. The record player. The empty potato chip bag. The beer cans. The ashtray, with Johnny's cigar still glowing.

"Well, this looks comfy," she said. "But where are the party hats and the noisemakers?"

She was wearing an ill-fitting, too-tight cotton dress, and I remembered it from the days when she was scurrying back and forth behind the lunch counter at Burke's. But now it looked as if her wardrobe had been supplemented from the closets of the Dunbars. The fraying blue cardigan she had on was so large it must have once belonged to Dr. Dunbar. It fell from her broad shoulders like drapery, hanging down to her thighs, and the sleeves were turned up multiple times. And she was wearing a pair of slippers that had been Mrs. Dunbar's.

"This isn't a party," Johnny said. "This is an antiparty."

"Sad," she said, nodding in understanding.

"We were invited to a party," I rushed to explain, "but we didn't want to go."

"Why the hell not?"

"You had to have a date," said Johnny.

"Gotcha." And then she flashed a smile that made her look as if she were preparing to take a bite out of something.

I had an impulse to say that we could have found dates if we wanted to, but I kept my mouth shut. That remark would only have made us seem more pathetic. Besides, upon her arrival the attic became the place I most wanted to spend New Year's Eve.

Johnny sat down in the children's chair, and Louisa sat where Johnny had been. She pointed to Johnny's record player, where Larry Kert's version of "Maria" emanated from the mesh-covered speaker. "You're sure wearing that out. I could hear it down in my room. What are you listening to?"

"*West Side Story*," said Johnny. "But this isn't the movie soundtrack. It's the original Broadway recording."

The distinction meant nothing to her. "Don't you ever play anything else?"

I reached down and picked up the stack of albums we'd brought to the party. "What do you want to hear? We've got Dave Brubeck. The Kingston Trio. The Brothers Four. Odetta."

"You have any Ricky Nelson?"

"Nope," Johnny answered. "Sorry."

"Bobby Vee?"

"No Bobby Vee."

She shrugged and pointed to the bottle at Johnny's feet. "What are you ringing in the New Year with?" Midnight was hours away.

"Blackberry brandy. Want a drink?"

"You have any more beers?"

"Sorry."

"Okay. What the hell."

"You want me to get you a glass?" offered Johnny.

Louisa laughed. "Don't bother." She reached for the bottle, twisted the top off, and then did exactly what a teenage boy would do: she wiped the rim with the palm of her hand.

After two swallows she grimaced and handed the brandy back to Johnny. "You could put that on pancakes." Nevertheless, after the bottle passed from Johnny to me, she accepted it when it came back to her.

For a long time no one said anything. We simply circulated the bottle and listened to Larry Kert and Carol Lawrence profess their doomed love. As Tony and Maria approached their fate, Johnny grew increasingly drunk. Louisa was visibly bored, and she didn't even know how the story ended. . . .

Louisa spoke up. "This must be a real fancy affair your folks went to tonight," she said to Johnny. "I saw the red dress your mom was wearing. Jesus, was that something!"

Johnny nodded. "They go to that dance every year. It goes on all night, and then when it's over the McDonoughs—they own the hotel—open up the restaurant and fix bacon and eggs for everybody."

The music was over, but no one got up to put on another record.

"But she won't wear that dress again next year, will she? It's a new dress every year, I'm sure."

"I don't know. Maybe."

"She'll probably wear it once, and then it'll end up over there." Louisa pointed to a standing wardrobe filled with garment bags.

"Could be."

"Damn fancy dress for this town," she observed. "Is your mom from Willow Falls?"

"Detroit. She and my dad met at the University of Michigan."

"How the hell did they end up here? A doctor—he can go anywhere."

Louisa may not have been from Willow Falls, but it hadn't taken her long to understand why so many people in our town worshipped Rex Dunbar. He wasn't like the mayor, whose family had become wealthy selling Chevrolets to the residents of Willow Falls for decades. Nor was he like L. D. Smalley, who had been drawing up deeds and writing wills in town for over thirty years, or Gordon Ruland, whose family had been selling groceries in Willow Falls almost as long as the town had been there. As admired as these and other men were, they were in Willow Falls because they were from there. But Rex Dunbar and his stylish, beautiful wife—as Louisa said, they could have gone anywhere.

"After my dad got out of the service," Johnny said, "he and my mom got in the car and took off. They were planning to drive out to the West Coast and take their time getting there. They stopped in Willow Falls for gas, and they liked the town right away. They thought it would be a good place to raise a family."

"To each his own," said Louisa, shrugging as if to suggest that while that might have been a reason good enough for the Dunbars, it didn't count for much with her. She pulled a crushed pack of Chesterfields from the pocket of her cardigan. "You sports have a light?"

Before I could grab the matches, Johnny picked them up and tossed them to Louisa. I would have lit her cigarette for her.

"You probably know how we landed here," she said. "Lester said he knew a fellow here who'd give him a job. Guess what. No fellow. No job."

The bottle came around to me again. I took what I believed to be an impressively long swallow and felt the brandy burn its way down my throat. Heat radiated throughout my chest, but that sensation didn't match the syrupy sweetness. I grimaced, then spoke up with false confidence. "I can't wait to get the hell out of Willow Falls."

"Yeah?" replied Louisa. "You have a destination in mind?"

"Not really. Chicago, maybe. The West Coast. Someplace far away, that's for sure."

"How about you?" she asked Johnny. "You looking to get out, too?"

"My dad thinks a small college would be a good fit for me. Someplace like Carleton—that's in Minnesota. Or maybe Macalester, in Saint Paul."

"That's what he thinks. . . . What do you think?"

"Sure, either of those would be okay."

She turned back to me. "But those aren't far enough away for you?"

"I'm not sure I'll wait until college to leave."

"Really?" She looked unconvinced.

"I might take off next summer. See if I can find a job somewhere. Out west, maybe. Like on a ranch."

"What the hell do you know about working on a ranch?" asked Louisa.

I shrugged. "I can learn."

"And break your damn back in the process."

"I'm not afraid of hard work."

"I grew up on a farm in North Dakota. I couldn't wait to get the hell out of there. Which is what my old man did. Left me and my mom holding the rope." She shook her head disapprovingly. "And you want to sign on for that kind of life? Thanks but no thanks."

Wounded though I was, I made an attempt to recover. "Ranch work is what I'd like to do."

"You think there's a difference? My mother died on the farm. Drowned in a spring flood, trying to save a cow."

"Sorry to hear that," said Johnny.

"Yeah. Well. We hadn't hardly been in touch for a while. If she hadn't owed so much on the place I might have got something out of it. Then I wouldn't have had to follow Lester and his big ideas."

As fascinating as I found Louisa's history, some of which I'd heard from my mother and other sources around town, it wasn't holding Johnny's interest. He wanted to return to something I'd said. "You mean," he said, his mouth and eyes all circles of astonishment, "you wouldn't even stick around for the summer after we graduate?"

I shrugged and looked over to Louisa as if to say, what can you do with these kids?

But Louisa's attention was drifting. She stood and walked over to one of the small attic windows. "Denver for me," she said, peering out the cobwebbed glass. "I got a cousin there."

"Yeah, Denver is cool," said Johnny.

But Louisa had already lost interest in geography. She poked around the attic's darker margins, casually inspecting the Dunbar family's artifacts. She picked up a gilt-framed sepia photograph of a fierce-looking white-bearded man. "Relative?" she asked Johnny.

"My mom's grandfather."

"Mean-looking old bastard."

"He was an Episcopalian minister. Mom said he was pretty strict. Not like her dad."

"I still think he looks like a mean bastard." Louisa cocked her head, as if she needed to consider him from another angle. "I lived with a minister's family once," she said, "while I was in high school. He was nothing but an old lecher. All short and shriveled and pockmarked. I think maybe he'd had smallpox. Anyway, he was sneaking around all the time, trying to catch me alone or undressing or something. And I was supposed to be grateful they took me in. They did it as a favor to my mom. She thought it was important for me to go to high school, and the town closest to our farm didn't have one. A high school, I mean." Louisa shuddered. "I should have told his wife about him spying on me. She was a fat old bitch and she hated me for some reason. But if I would've told on her husband I bet she'd have killed him."

Louisa continued her tour of the attic. When she came to a sewing machine she wiped a finger through the dust that covered it. "This work?"

"I guess."

"And it's just sitting up here gathering dust. Must be nice."

Louisa grabbed the handle of a baby carriage and rolled it a few feet back and forth. "Shouldn't there be two of these?"

"There were. My mom gave one to her sister. But she wanted to keep this one. Because it was mine, she said. And because it came from a company in England."

Louisa wheeled the carriage out of the shadows and toward us. "Mrs. Dunbar and her beautiful baby boy . . . I bet the two of you made quite a sight rolling around Willow Falls."

"I remember those days well," said Johnny with a smile. I could tell by the way his head rolled from side to side on the chair back that he was drunk. "Didn't have a care in the world. Just laid on my back staring up at the sky. Let someone else do the driving."

Louisa laughed. "You remember when you were a baby? Like hell."

"Yep, those were the good old days."

Johnny rose unsteadily to his feet and handed me the brandy. There wasn't much left in the bottle. He made his way slowly over toward Louisa. He looked tenderly into the carriage, as if he expected to find his infant self inside. Then he turned around and flopped backward into the carriage. It wobbled and bounced on its springs, but somehow it didn't collapse or fall over.

Louisa braced herself and held tight to the handle. "Christ!"

I struggled out of the rocking chair. By the time I arrived at the carriage, Johnny was settling in, his legs hanging over the side.

"What the hell are you doing?"

Johnny imitated a baby's cry in response, a series of evenly spaced "wah-wah-wah's."

I looked up at Louisa. "I think he wants his bottle."

"Better give it to him." Her laugh was as throaty and deep as a man's. "So long as I don't have to nurse him!"

At that Johnny's crying intensified, and he reached for Louisa.

"Quick," she said, "give him the damn bottle!"

I thrust the bottle at him, but when Johnny brought it to his mouth, most of the liquor just spilled down his chin. Then he gagged and coughed, spraying blackberry brandy all over himself.

I took the bottle from him. To Louisa I said, "That wasn't the answer."

"We'll take him for a walk." With that, she wheeled the carriage around and began to push Johnny toward the attic's darker end. I hurried to catch up so I could walk alongside Louisa.

As he rolled over the attic's uneven boards, Johnny bounced in the carriage and shouted gleefully, "Whee! Whee!"

Since they were heading toward the stairs, I ran ahead and spread my arms wide, as if the carriage was out of control and needed to be blocked. Louisa misunderstood my intent and thought I was there to catch Johnny. She gave the carriage a hard shove, but even with Johnny's wobbling weight, the wheels rolled true.

With the extra momentum provided by its heavy load, the carriage bumped hard into my hands. "Hang on!" I told Johnny, and ran a few steps before sending him back on his way to Louisa.

She crouched to catch him. "Come to Momma!"

Back and forth we went, until well beyond the point where Johnny was enjoying the experience. And then he rose up—or tried to—and said, "Stop, stop! I . . . I need . . ."

He tried to climb out of the carriage, causing it to topple over and crash. Johnny tumbled out, landing hard. And then he pushed himself up onto his hands and knees just in time to throw up a foul, purple, potato chip-flecked liquid.

"Oh, shit!" exclaimed Louisa.

Johnny's back arched over and over with the force of his retching. Finally, the coughing and convulsing stopped. He almost pitched forward into his own vomit, but somehow he managed to roll over onto his back.

"Oh no you don't," said Louisa. "Sit up! Up, up!" She reached for him, and Johnny lifted his arms toward her limply.

She grabbed his wrists and pulled him up roughly. Then she let go of Johnny slowly, waiting to see if he'd collapse again. He didn't.

"How about you?" Louisa asked me. "You going to lose your lunch, too?"

The fetid stench of vomit filled the air, but my stomach held. "Not me."

"Hey," said Johnny, "I missed the basket."

"You sure did," I replied. "But you hit damn near everything else."

"If you think you're finished," Louisa said to Johnny, "I'll go get the bucket and mop."

"I am . . . finished," Johnny said with the gesture of an umpire calling a runner safe.

"Why the hell," Louisa said, pinching her nostrils, "did I ever let myself think I was done cleaning up puke?"

"I know where the mop is," I said. "I'll go get it."

"Forget it," said Louisa, heading toward the stairs. "I'm still in practice."

She started down the steps, then stopped suddenly. I could hear the attic door creak open.

"I thought I heard something up here." It was Dr. Dunbar.

Louisa must not have been very drunk, for she seemed to ascend the steps backward without any difficulty. At the top, she continued to back up, situating herself in such a way as to block Dr. Dunbar's view of his drunken son. She wrapped the cardigan around herself as she did so.

Wearing a hat and overcoat still, the doctor stepped up into the attic. "Celebrating 1963 a little early, are we?" he said with a laugh.

His smile vanished, however, once he saw the overturned baby carriage and smelled the vomit and cigar smoke. Dr. Dunbar peered around Louisa into the darkness, where his son now sat on his haunches under the attic's low ceiling. "Johnny? What the hell is going on up here?"

"Hap-Pee New Year!" said Johnny.

As if he knew immediately that his son would not be

able to provide a coherent explanation for what had happened, Dr. Dunbar turned to Louisa and me.

"I was on my way to get something to clean up the mess," Louisa said meekly.

That left me to explain, but Johnny saved me by struggling to his feet just in time.

"Are you all right?" Dr. Dunbar asked his son.

"I will be," Johnny said, listing unsteadily from side to side.

It made me dizzy to watch Johnny teetering, and I had to look away.

Dr. Dunbar walked over to the carriage and lifted it upright. He rolled it back and forth a few feet, as if it were important to make certain it was still operating properly. Then he walked the length of the attic slowly, like a general inspecting his troops. He stopped and stared down at the record player, as if it—rather than the beer cans or brandy bottle or brimming ashtray—would provide some final answer.

He tilted his hat back and then turned abruptly. "I have to drive out to the Preston place. That's why I came home. Mr. Preston called and said his wife is having abdominal pains. Louisa, can you help Johnny get into bed?"

She nodded.

"And Matthew, you won't be spending the night here. If you're not sober enough to walk home, I'll give you a ride."

"I can walk," I said.

"You might want to tell your mother about this little escapade. She'll hear about it in any case. I'll be talking to her tomorrow. So think very carefully about what you say."

"Okay."

My response must have sounded flippant. "Okay?" the doctor replied. "You're damn right it's 'okay.' Now get the hell out of here. Your New Year's celebration is over."

After the attic's musty gloom, entering the well-lit halls of the Dunbar house was like stepping into sunlight, and that instant clarity alerted me to the fact that I was drunker than I'd realized. I couldn't tarry, however. Dr. Dunbar would soon be coming down the stairs, and I had no desire for another confrontation.

I pulled on my overshoes and buttoned my coat as quickly as I could, but when I walked out the door, Dr. Dunbar was already there, standing beside his Chrysler, his medical bag in hand.

"You sure you don't want a ride, Matt? It's twenty below." Although his words were issued in icy little clouds, his tone was more gentle than it had been in the attic.

"That's okay. It's not that far."

"You might think what you were doing tonight was real grown-up, but trust me, it wasn't. On your walk home you might give some thought not only to what you'll tell your mother about your shenanigans tonight, but about what it means to be a man. Because judging from tonight's behavior, Matthew, you have a long way to go. A hell of a long way."

No doubt the doctor was right. I should have used the distance I had to travel to contemplate the defects in my character. But I had only reached the bottom of the Dunbar's long driveway when I felt compelled to look back up at the place I had just been banished from.

The house's Victorian architecture—its chimney, dormers, tower, and turret—gave it a looming, jagged silhouette against the moonlit sky. Most of the windows were dark, but the two tall rectangles that were Johnny's bedroom windows glowed faintly. I chose to believe that Louisa had left a light on for Johnny so that when the room began to spin like the wheels on a baby carriage he could find a spot to focus on and thereby slow the revolutions.

Dr. Dunbar was right in a sense. I did want to be a man, with all accompanying powers and privileges. But I also wanted Louisa Lindahl to tuck me into bed, and right now that seemed more likely to happen to a little boy.

7.

WHEN MY MOTHER WOKE AT NOON on New Year's Day, I asked what she'd recommend for a hangover. I didn't explain why I wanted to know, and she didn't ask.

"Aspirin and Pepto-Bismol," she said. "Good for the stomach and for the head." My mother specialized in practical lessons that helped with the rigors of daily living. Airy, abstract advice on setting life goals or finding happiness was not for her. *Aspirin and Pepto-Bismol.* That was classic Esther Garth. And asking for her hangover cure constituted my confession of my New Year's Eve misbehavior. After that, I no longer worried about the doctor's call. Not that I'd been especially concerned. My mother might well have told the doctor that he could go to hell, and that she didn't need his or anyone else's help in raising her son.

But while the prospect of my mother's anger didn't distress me, the possibility of never entering the Dunbar home again did. Following my New Year's Eve expulsion I believed that was quite possible, and as the first days of 1963 came and went with no word from my friend or his family, my anxiety increased. What I felt was more than worry, more like an alteration of my being. In English class we'd just finished a unit on Greek and Roman mythology, and I felt as if I were living my own variation on the myth of Antaeus. I had to be back in the Dunbar home in order not to be diminished.

Fortunately, before a week was out Johnny phoned and invited me to come over. The science project we'd been collaborating on for weeks would soon be due, and we were far from finished.

"I don't think your dad would appreciate having me around," I said.

"Nah, he won't mind. He's not mad anymore. Besides, he and Mom won't be here. They're taking the twins to the Saint Bartholomew's Carnival."

"You're sure?"

"I'm sure. Now get your ass over here."

Despite Johnny's assurances, I still had my doubts. When I rang the doorbell and Dr. Dunbar answered, I was prepared to be sent back the way I came.

"Come in, Matthew, come in," he said. "Johnny's in the kitchen. Or what was the kitchen. I believe it's been converted to an anatomy lab." Nothing in his demeanor suggested that he wasn't pleased to see me.

Johnny had laid out poster board on the kitchen table, along with paper, clay, colored pencils, small bottles of model car paints, a portable typewriter, scissors, tape, glue, and a few of his father's medical books. For our project we planned to capitalize on our reputations as doctors-to-be, and depict ways that major organs could fatally malfunction. Johnny was a talented artist, and he'd drawn on the poster a body with arrows and labels listing the location of major organs. I had some skill with modeling clay, and I molded miniatures of a few organs, both healthy and diseased. We planned to glue these to the poster or arrange them on their own cardboard plaques. Labels would offer brief descriptions of the organ and the symptoms and consequences of disease. The project was an elaborate and visual analogue of the thought I'd had when Dr. Dunbar informed me of my father's death. *I know where the spleen is, do you?*

"I've seen operating rooms that weren't as messy," Dr. Dunbar said as we surveyed the kitchen.

Johnny tossed me a lump of clay. "Make me a liver."

"With or without cirrhosis?"

"With," Johnny said. "Definitely with."

"I would think," said Dr. Dunbar, "that you two would want to avoid that topic. At least in my presence."

Johnny laughed at the remark.

Mrs. Dunbar came into the kitchen wearing her fur coat. "There's cold chicken in the fridge. Or heat up a pizza if you'd prefer. I know it's futile to ask you to clear off the table when you're finished, but if you could at least leave enough room for us to have breakfast tomorrow that would be much appreciated."

"Genius," said Johnny, "likes things messy."

"Really?" said Mrs. Dunbar. "Well, I'm sure your sisters would prefer not to stare at a model of a perforated bowel while they eat their Cheerios."

"Genius can't be rushed either."

"And did you explain that to Mr. Lannon when he gave you a due date for your project?" asked Dr. Dunbar.

"He'll understand."

"Don't be too sure of that."

The twins came in wearing their matching red wool coats. As a concession to individuality, however, Janet wore white furry earmuffs and Julia a blue knitted cap.

"What kind of cake do you want?" Julia asked Johnny. "We'll get you any kind you like."

This was no empty promise. Every year at Saint Bartholomew's Carnival the twins bought ticket after ticket at the cakewalk. And their perseverance always paid off. The previous year they brought home five cakes.

"Chocolate," said Johnny, "with chocolate frosting."

"Hey," I added, "don't I get to put in an order?"

"Oh Matt. Everyone knows you'll eat anything."

Did they? I didn't even know that about myself.

"Remember," said Mrs. Dunbar, guiding the twins out the door and then linking her arm in her husband's. "Cold chicken in the refrigerator."

Halfway out the door, the doctor turned back to us to add with a smile, "And I don't want to come home to the smell of cigars."

As soon as they left, I questioned Johnny about what had happened after I was kicked out of the house, both that night and in the days since.

"I don't remember much," Johnny said. "After I fell out of the baby buggy, everything's sort of a blank. When I woke up the next day I didn't feel too bad. Thirsty as hell, but that was about it. No headache. No upset stomach. Then I had a bowl of soup and I puked my guts out again."

"What about Louisa putting you to bed? What was that like?"

"Damned if I know. I woke up in my own bed, but I don't remember how I got there."

"Were you dressed? Under the covers?"

"Dressed. Except for my shoes. Someone had put a quilt over me and a pan next to the bed. But it could have been my dad or mom who did that."

"She hasn't said anything to you since?"

"I've hardly seen her."

"Is she in trouble with your folks?"

"Not that I know of." He pushed a lump of clay in my direction. "What if we just painted a lung black for lung cancer?"

"Wouldn't that be black lung? That's a different thing."

"Maybe we could have just one model for all the lung problems? Emphysema. Black lung. Cancer."

"That'd work. Are they all fatal?"

"They've got to be, don't they?"

"I guess." I rolled the clay between my palm. "Your parents didn't ground you or anything?"

"They gave me the talk. You know, we're disappointed in you, we expect better from you, we hope you've learned something. . . ."

I wanted to know whether my name came up during the course of that talk, but before I could ask him, Johnny turned back to the poster board. "I think the models of the organs should be to the same scale as the drawing. So it looks like they've just been removed."

"Or could be put back."

"Yeah, like you'd want to put a diseased liver back."

"Well, if there's no hope . . ."

The Dunbar house had a narrow staircase that led from

the floor above down to the pantry off the kitchen. They called it the maid's staircase, though the Dunbars had never employed anyone in that capacity. Coming down into the kitchen through that entrance enabled Louisa to arrive without our having heard or seen her approach. We looked up, and she was there.

Without a word of greeting, she walked over to the sink and filled a glass of water from the tap. She was dressed exactly as she had been on New Year's Eve, right down to the slippers. After she drank, she leaned back, crossed her arms, and watched us as intently as we watched her. She seemed bored but a little on edge, as if even a quarrel would be a welcome distraction.

"Don't mind me," she said finally. "Go ahead with whatever you were doing."

"A science project," Johnny explained.

"Yeah? Looks like you're performing a—what do you call it?—an autopsy."

"Nope," said Johnny. "The patient is still alive."

She came over to the table and looked down at our unfinished work. "Maybe you should call in a specialist."

"Won't do any good," I said. "He's doomed."

"Might as well sew him up and send him on his way then." Louisa bent over and looked closely at me. "The doctor sure did a nice job with *your* stitches." She touched her own eyebrow.

I pointed to her midsection. "How'd he do with yours?"

She set down her water glass, backed up from the table, bent over, and grabbed the hem of her dress. While Johnny and I watched in disbelief, Louisa Lindahl slowly pulled and gathered up material until her dress rose above her knees, above her pale thighs, above her once-white-now-graying cotton underpants, above that navel into which my fingertip had once inserted itself, and still higher, until the scar that traversed her abdomen was exposed, a puckered pink slash that looked more like a healed-over knife wound than a bullet's track. She let us gape for a moment—not knowing that she had been bared to us previously in a similar way—and then she dropped her dress and smoothed it down the front.

This little act apparently provided the amusement she'd been seeking. Louisa clapped her hands and laughed. "You are a pair, you know that? You should see the look on your faces!"

Johnny and I glanced quickly at each other as if to verify what she had seen. His face was pure amazement.

"Well?" Louisa asked. "Did you want to look or didn't you?"

"He did a nice job," I said. "Wouldn't you say, Johnny? Your dad did a nice job?"

"He knows how to pull a stitch tight, that's for sure."

Only seconds had passed, but I was already making demands on my memory. Had I seen a mound at the front of her underpants, a springy little swelling underneath the fabric? Had an inch or two of cotton torn away from the elastic waistband and left a triangle of flesh uncovered? If she had only given us some warning, I would have known to focus even more carefully.

Louisa walked over to the refrigerator and opened it. "Suppose anyone would notice if one of these beers went missing?"

"They'd notice," said Johnny. "But they'd blame me."

"Or me," I added.

Still peering around the refrigerator's interior, Louisa replied, "Really? I thought you two were brandy drinkers."

"Beer, when we can get it," I said.

"When you can get it?"

"A couple guys will buy for us sometimes," Johnny said. "But they're not always around. It's kind of hit or miss."

She closed the refrigerator. "Hell. I'll buy you all the beer you want."

"Are you serious?" Johnny threw down his pencil. "What are we sitting around here for? Let's go."

"Now?" said Louisa. "All right. What the hell. Let me get my coat."

Before she exited the kitchen, she paused in the doorway. "They're just underpants, you know. Everyone wears them."

"But not everyone has a bullet wound," said Johnny.

## 8.

LOUISA LEANED FORWARD TO TURN the radio dial. She was trying to steady the signal from Fargo's KFRG, but just when it seemed as if the Four Seasons' high harmonies had finally found their way to us, Johnny would turn a corner or round a curve and the radio would resume its guttural hiss.

When Louisa wasn't cursing the radio reception she was complaining about the lack of heat in the Plymouth Valiant. The car was officially Johnny's mother's, but he was free to take it anytime the keys were hanging on the hook next to the back door. I had similar privileges with our old DeSoto, but since my mother usually drove the car to work, I seldom had access to it in the evening.

We were shoulder to shoulder in the compact car, and every time Louisa shivered I felt it. "If there's any heat coming out down there," she said, waving her foot back and forth under the dashboard, "I sure as hell don't feel it."

"I need to keep the defroster running full blast a little longer," explained Johnny, as he rubbed the heel of his gloved hand at the frost forming on the windshield. We were on our way to a little roadside tavern about five miles outside town. Louisa didn't want someone in a liquor store or bar in town seeing her carry a case of beer out to a car that looked like Mrs. Dunbar's.

"By the way," said Louisa, "the guys who usually buy your liquor for you—how much do you pay them?"

She looked to Johnny first. He didn't answer, and I knew why. But what were we thinking?—that she offered to do this because she was so fond of us? "Sometimes we give them a six-pack," I said. "If it's a big order."

"A six-pack. Gee." Louisa huddled deeper inside her plaid wool mackinaw. It was another ill-fitting garment, but in this case it occurred to me that its original owner had probably been Lester Huston.

"It's usually someone's older brother," Johnny added. "But we'll pay you. What's fair?"

"I don't know. A case of beer . . . Five bucks?"

"What do you think, Matt? Five okay with you?"

"Sure, fine. I'll kick in." I knew if I didn't agree, Johnny would pay it all himself.

Louisa pointed toward the glowing blue neon of a Hamm's beer sign on the right side of the road ahead. "There it is. Just pull into the lot and leave the engine running. Maybe the car will be warm by the time I come out."

Before she got out of the car, we each gave her five dollars.

"Okay," she said, pocketing the bills. "And you said Budweiser?"

"Or Schlitz."

About five minutes later, Louisa Lindahl exited the Red Hawk Bar with a case of Blue Lake Lager, everyone's beer of last resort. "This was what they had cold," she explained. "I thought we could have a few before we go back to the house. Unless you have to get right back to your homework." She offered no change from the purchase.

"As long as I'm home before my folks and the twins get back from the carnival," Johnny replied cheerfully.

"I've got all night," I added.

"So let's go," said Louisa. "You know some out-of-the-way place we can park?"

Before he put the car in gear, I knew where Johnny would take us.

Johnny stopped just short of the pine trees that seemed planted to hide the entrance to Frenchman's Forest. We were not far from the clearing where Lester Huston and Louisa Lindahl had lived together in their ramshackle cabin. I knew he'd drive to the Forest, but I didn't know he'd choose a spot as loaded with memory as those pine boughs were laden with snow.

Louisa recognized the significance of the site, but it didn't appear to present any emotional difficulty for her. As soon as the car was parked, she twisted herself around, got up on her knees, and reached over into the backseat to pull out bottles of beer for each of us.

I had a moment of panic, but she pulled a church key out of her pocket, and opened each of the bottles in turn. Then, after a long pull at her beer, Louisa said, "Lester . . . You know why he wanted to live here? In the woods, I mean."

"Because it was cheap?" replied Johnny.

"Lester thought he'd be able to hunt for our food. 'These woods are full of game,' he'd say. No shit. Raccoons ate our garbage, and every morning I'd see deer outside our bedroom window. But they were safe from Lester. The only gun he had was that little .22. Not that he could hit a goddamn thing." She laughed and patted her stomach. "I mean, obviously. The sonofabitch damn near missed me at point-blank range."

"Yeah, I've been meaning to ask," Johnny said. "What does it feel like to get shot?" Sometimes his naïveté brought him effortlessly to just the right question.

Louisa leaned away from Johnny, as if she needed a little distance to see who was asking her such a question. "It hurt like hell. But you didn't need me to tell you that, did you?"

"Like being burned?"

"Just trust me: you don't want to get shot."

"Do you miss him? Lester?"

"Hell, no. You don't miss someone who tried to kill you, for Chrissake."

Johnny's questions emboldened me to ask, "Why'd he try to shoot you?"

"Not try. He did shoot me. I showed you the god-damn scar. Because he thought I should have fixed him a Thanksgiving dinner that was more substantial than a bowl of soup. You bring something more than soup home, I told him, and I'll fix it. Like pointing a gun at me was going to make a Thanksgiving feast magically appear on the table. Lester Huston . . . Good riddance, I say. Hey, turn that up." She pointed to the radio. "Telstar," a chart-topping instrumental by the Tornados, was playing. I was sick of the song, but I did as she said.

"Now, is that supposed to be a real satellite signal in the song?" Louisa asked. "I thought I heard that somewhere."

"It's guitars," I said.

She twisted herself around again, but this time it was merely to make herself more comfortable. She lifted her legs, extended them across Johnny's lap, and rested her back against me. Then she reached over, turned up the radio, and settled back to listen to the song. When it was over, Louisa asked, "Do you ever park here with your girls? I know this is a big make-out spot. Lester used to complain that we couldn't get back out to the road some nights because love cars were blocking the road. That's what he called them. Love cars."

"I have," I said. "A few times."

Johnny leaned forward. "Yeah? With Debbie?"

"Ooh, Debbie—she sounds cute. Does she look like Debbie Reynolds?"

"She has brown hair. That's about as far as it goes."

"And why aren't you with her tonight? Because you had to work on your science project?"

"We broke up."

"I bet I know why. She wouldn't get in the backseat with you."

"Because I fixed her soup for Thanksgiving."

"Oooo . . . That's very good. Nasty, but good. Now give us the juicy details about what the two of you did in your love car."

I regretted having brought up the subject, and I wasn't going to make matters worse by going into detail about what Debbie McCarren and I did or didn't do when we parked on the edge of Frenchman's Forest. Nor would I tell them that the last time we were here, on a windy autumn night when sleet struck the car like the clicking of impatient fingernails, we didn't spend hours with our tongues in each other's mouths and my hand inside her unbuttoned blouse. Instead, I just sat behind the wheel with my hands to myself while Debbie went through the reasons we could no longer be a couple. "You push too hard," was a phrase I heard more than once that night, referring primarily to my sexual advances. "Why can't you let things be the way they are?" she asked. "Why do you always want more, more, more?" I didn't have a good answer because I couldn't really understand the question. Who didn't want more?

Louisa pushed herself back against me. "Come on. Did you even get past first base with her?"

"A gentleman doesn't talk about such things."

Louisa burst out laughing. "Ooh, that's rich! A gentleman! Too bad Debbie can't hear you say that. She might even let you do everything you want. And as long as we're on the subject," she went on, "let me give you two a tip. When you're parking with a girl in the winter, leave the car running. I mean, obviously. You need to keep the heat on. She won't give anything up if she's freezing. And you want the radio playing, too."

In order to accommodate Louisa's semiprone position across the front seat, I had put my arm up along the back of it. And now while she was talking I let my arm drop, knowing that my hand would fall near her breast, padded as it was beneath several layers of clothing. What did I have to lose? After all, Louisa didn't believe in gentlemen anyway. . . .

When my hand landed where I hoped it would, Louisa didn't startle or stop talking. But with an alacrity that indicated she had expected this move all along, she lifted my hand and put it back on the seat. She could not have plucked a piece of lint from her clothing with greater detachment or deliberation. "But make sure the tailpipe isn't in the snow," she continued. "Because if that happens, carbon monoxide will back up into the car. I heard about that happening once, and the guy and the girl were both killed. There. Don't say you didn't learn anything tonight."

It wasn't what I'd hoped to learn about lovers in parked cars, but then her own experiences in Frenchman's Forest probably produced more mixed emotions for Lousia Lindahl.

"You have any more advice for us?" I asked.

She sat up a little straighter. "Since you asked." She took a long pull from her bottle of Blue Lake and said, "If you're going to go fast, go faster. And if you're going to go slow, go slower."

"What the hell's that supposed to mean?" asked Johnny.

She pushed back against me again. "Should I tell him?"

My first thought on hearing her advice was simple: who wants to go slow? But if I asked that, it would only prove that I didn't have any idea what Louisa was talking about, and that wouldn't do. Instead I said, as nonchalantly as possible, "Might as well."

She was silent for a long moment, while a commercial for a Fargo Ford dealer played on the radio. "What the hell," she said finally. "He'll know when the time comes."

"Fine," said Johnny. "Be that way."

A long silence followed. It felt as if we were all waiting

for something to fill the moment, but we were also all equally unsure of what that might be.

Johnny finally spoke up, and I wasn't happy to hear what he had to say. "We should get back."

Louisa finished her beer in one long swig, then replied, "Okay, let's skedaddle." She swung her legs off Johnny's lap, and he put the car in reverse. Soon we were out from under the dark shelter of the trees. The winter sky was bright with stars.

We had to cache the beer someplace, and I volunteered our garage. My mother was working, and I could hide what was left of the case under a canvas tarp against the back wall. The beer wouldn't be found there and it probably wouldn't freeze.

Johnny drove to my house. He pulled into the driveway, and I unloaded the beer from the backseat and carried it into the garage through the side door. I wanted to be sure old Mrs. Darden didn't see what I was doing.

While I was covering the bottles of beer, I heard Johnny back the car out of the driveway. I ran out of the garage, but only in time to see the Valiant's taillights fading into the night. I was shocked, as I'd assumed all along that after the beer was hidden we would all return to the Dunbar house, and that Johnny and I would resume working on our science project, as strange as that schoolboy activity might seem at this point.

A misunderstanding, I told myself, but that didn't make me feel much better. I suppose I could have pulled my stocking cap down over my ears and buttoned my coat and set

out for the Dunbars'. If I ran I would arrive there only minutes after they did. But I didn't. Instead, I took two bottles of
beer and carried them into the house.

I didn't bother turning on the lights in my room. I just
sat down on the bed and drank my cheap beer. When I
turned on the radio, that fucking song was playing again.
But now the guitars sounded more like the high, nasal
taunts of the playground than signals beamed down from
space.

## 9.

I'D HOPED THAT THE REMAINING BOTTLES of Blue Lake Lager would go the way of the first three, but since such a set of circumstances was unlikely to arise again, I could hardly argue for saving the beer when another occasion arose. Otis Unwin's parents were leaving town for a few days, and so he would have the house to himself. He didn't want to throw a full-scale party—he was worried that the neighbors would call his parents or the sheriff or both—but Otis did invite a few friends, including Johnny and me, over for a weekend of poker and beer. And so one Friday evening not long after our outing to Frenchman's Forest with Louisa, Johnny picked me up and we drove to Otis Unwin's along with nineteen bottles of Blue Lake Lager.

Our arrival completed the short guest list. Only ten of us were in attendance, a small gathering, as Otis had hoped for. The poker game had already started, and Johnny sat in. I joined the rest of the kibitzers standing a safe distance behind the players.

Johnny and I and some of the other fellows in Otis's kitchen played poker often, and we took the game seriously.

Our preferred game was stud, either five- or seven-card, and we scorned wild-card or split-pot games. We didn't show hole cards when the privilege wasn't paid for. If a player ran out of money he was finished for the night; there were no loans at the table. The stakes were quarter, dime, nickel, with a limit of three raises, and while that might not seem like much, it was still possible to win or lose enough over the course of an evening to make a difference to your wallet or your spirits for days to come. Outsiders occasionally sat in on the game, and they invariably lost. They drank too much or they didn't keep track of the cards, they couldn't stand to fold or they called bets they shouldn't have, they chased pots or their faces gave away their good hands and their bluffs, and often they relied more on luck than on skill. We called those interlopers "squirrels," though not to their faces.

Not long after he sat down, Johnny had the largest stack of chips on the table. This was not a surprise. Of our group of regulars, he was acknowledged to be the best player. He was good at math and could figure odds quickly. He didn't have a poker face, but there was another reason he couldn't be read—he never stopped laughing and talking and taunting the other players. He kept up a running commentary on the cards and how players were likely to play them. The passivity he displayed in every other kind of competition was absent from the poker table. He had no trouble at all taking another player's last nickel.

But what really distinguished Johnny as a player was his understanding that money wasn't money in poker. For him it was merely a way to keep score, a tool to be used in playing a game, much like a racket, bat, or ball. On more than one occasion he'd said to me, "You play poker with money, Matt, not cards." And with that remark he identified exactly what prevented me from being a better player. I couldn't get past the fact that chips represented money, and that made me a conservative player. I seldom bluffed, I folded all but the surest hands, and I didn't know how to buy pots or sandbag players into playing hands they shouldn't. I usually won for other reasons, to be sure, but in contrast to Johnny, my winnings were modest. In any case, I'd decided not to sit in on the game at Otis's because I wanted to drink more than a single beer, something I'd never do if I were playing.

There was a player that night who wasn't one of the regulars, but he was no squirrel. Tim Van Dine's older brother, Glen, had flunked out of Moorhead State College, and he was back in Willow Falls, pumping gas at the Mobil station and waiting until fall, when he'd enroll in a junior college and try to get his grades up so he could return to the university. Glen had played a lot of poker at his fraternity house, and his skill showed. His pile of chips was almost as large as Johnny's, but in contrast to Johnny, who chattered as much as an infielder during the game, Glen Van Dine said next to nothing. He wouldn't even announce called or raised bets; he simply tossed his chips into the pot. He knocked on the table to indicate a check, and he shoved his folded cards away as if he could barely stand to touch them. And when he had a winning hand he turned over his cards, pulled in the chips, and began to sort and stack them, all without saying a word.

It was close to ten o'clock when Gary Krynicki returned from the garage where the beers that wouldn't fit in the refrigerator were chilling. "Hey, there's a carload of girls out in the driveway," Gary announced. "Mary Gwynn, Bonnie Wahl, and Daniels and McCarren. They want to come in."

"No!" shouted Otis, jumping up from the card game. "Jesus, if this gets out of hand . . ."

While most of us would have welcomed the girls, it was Otis's party, so no one tried to argue with him when he went out to shoo them away.

Minutes later, Otis returned. "Garth? Debbie wants to talk to you. I think she's drunk, but I told her I'd give you the message. You can go out there if you like, but they can't come in. Got that?"

"Shit," I said. Then I finished my beer and walked out into the cold without bothering with a coat.

As soon as she saw me coming, Debbie rolled down the back window of Mary Gwynn's father's cream-colored Oldsmobile. She leaned out and waved, as if she were trying to catch my eye from a great distance. When I arrived at the car, however, Jilly Daniels pushed her way in front of Debbie in order to issue a warning on behalf of her friend. "Matt, don't say anything that'll hurt her. Really—"

"*I'm* not supposed to hurt *her*? Who do you think—Oh, forget it. Hey, Debbie."

Debbie extended a mittened hand in my direction. "Matt, I miss y-o-o-o-u-u!"

She was drunk, all right. I'd only seen her in that condition once before, at a party after the Homecoming Dance, but I remembered the signs. Debbie McCarren was vivacious and seldom had trouble making her moods and feelings known. But after a few drinks every expression of emotion seemed artificial and overwrought. Now, for example, she had furrowed her brow and pursed her lips in an attempt to look sad, but the effect was closer to a little girl's pout, and an unconvincing one at that. That said, her mascara was smeared as if she had been crying, and her cat's-eye glasses were askew. Her dark brown hair, usually lacquered into a smooth helmet, was mussed as well.

I used the cold as an excuse to jam my hands into my pockets. "Do you?"

"I mean it, Matty. I do." She leaned even farther out the window, and Jilly pretended to attempt to pull her back into the car. From the front seat, smart-ass Bonnie Wahl said over her shoulder, "*Matty*? That's cute."

"Shut up," Debbie snapped at her friend. "Can we talk, Matt? Please?"

"About what?"

"About us."

"I didn't think there was an 'us.'"

A light snow was falling, and Debbie batted at the flakes as if they were the only obstacle to agreement between us. "Please, Matt? In private?"

The Valiant was parked around the corner, and I nodded in its direction. "We can talk in Johnny's car."

Debbie scrambled out of the car and immediately linked her arm in mine.

Before we could walk away, Bonnie Wahl asked, "What the hell are we supposed to do?"

Debbie shrugged and said demurely, "You can go."

Jilly Daniels leaned out the window again. "Hey, Matt.

If we can't go in, can you at least bring some beer out? We'll pay."

"Sorry. Our supplies are limited."

"Oh, who needs them," said Bonnie. "We still have some vodka left."

Debbie McCarren was short, full-breasted, and wide-hipped, and she walked with a kind of waddle. She had large brown eyes, a pug nose, and an upper lip more prominent than the lower. She never would have been mistaken for beautiful, but somehow she worked what she had to her advantage. Or at least it worked for me, and Debbie knew as much.

Once we were ensconced in the Valiant, she scooted across the backseat and, in contrast to the way Louisa Lindahl had brusquely removed my hand from her body, Debbie pulled my arm around her and fitted herself snugly to my side. "Doesn't this feel . . . right?" Her breath smelled like vegetable soup mixed with rubbing alcohol. "What if we never broke up? What would we be doing tonight?"

I didn't know what to say. First of all, we hadn't broken up. Debbie McCarren had dropped me. Second, we likely would have been doing exactly what we had been doing—playing poker and drinking beer in my case, riding around with a pack of girls and handing a bottle of vodka back and forth in hers. And if we had passed on those activities for each other's company, we almost surely would have been doing exactly what we were doing now—seeking each other's heat in a parked car.

Debbie proceeded as if I had already answered. "And

would we be going to the Frost Festival Dance tomorrow night?"

I knew then what this reconciliation was all about. I pulled her closer, and she rose to meet my kiss with all the old familiar ardor and intensity.

After a few minutes of running our tongues around each other's mouths, I decided to test the depth and sincerity of her renewed fond feelings for me.

Trying to negotiate around and under coat, muffler, sweater, blouse, and brassiere seemed too complicated. It also presented too many opportunities for Debbie to stop me along the way. So I opted for a different route. I slid my hand up her skirt, high up her thigh. I was surprised she didn't immediately grab my hand or clamp her legs together to halt my progress. She squirmed under my touch, and while she might have been trying to wriggle away from my exploring fingers, it was also possible that she was writhing with passion. I chose to accept the latter interpretation.

Thanks to the hours Johnny and I had spent poring over Dr. Dunbar's anatomy books, I was pretty familiar with the parts and purposes of female genitalia. Unfortunately, however, I had no such familiarity with their undergarments. While I might have known what to do if my hand had been inside Debbie's girdle, I was baffled now, and I couldn't do anything but probe and poke dumbly around its tightly banded borders.

My quest soon came to an end in any case. Debbie's first "no" was spoken in the middle of a kiss, and because she said the word right into my mouth, it was almost completely unintelligible. Then she deftly rolled her hips in a way that made it imperative for me to remove my hand from between her legs.

"God," she said, breaking away from our embrace and sliding back across the seat. "I might have known. Here I am thinking about all the wonderful, romantic times we had together, and all you care about is what you can get. You haven't changed a bit."

Not changed? How could she say that? I'd seen Louisa Lindahl's bare breasts. I'd gotten drunk with her. She'd lifted her dress to show me her scar. She'd even advised me on what I should do in the backseat with a girl like Debbie. How could I not be changed?

Debbie tried to make a dramatic exit, but the door handle wouldn't cooperate. And as she yanked ineffectually on it, she became increasingly angry. "And to think I told Art Graber that I couldn't go to Frost Festival with him. Art Graber, for Chrissake!"

I reached across to help her with the door, and this prompted Debbie to fling her arm out violently in my direction. I pulled back, and she almost slid to the floor of the Valiant. But somehow something in that contortion caused the door to pop open, and Debbie scrambled out, trying to recompose herself in the process.

She must have felt that she hadn't adequately expressed her disgust, for she leaned back into the car's interior. "Another thing, Matthew, Matthew *Garth . . .*" She spoke my last name as if giving voice to it was a sufficient curse. But then her vocabulary failed her and she had to settle for something less subtle. "Oh, fuck you. Just fuck you!"

I watched Debbie McCarren walk away through the scrim of the falling snow. It was not quite as reckless a departure as it might have seemed. Both she and Bonnie Wahl lived less than three blocks from Otis Unwin.

I hadn't been in the best of moods when the evening began. In my mind the remaining Blue Lake Lager belonged to Louisa, Johnny, and me. We were supposed to drink it together, and I begrudged sharing it with the guys. And then just when I felt finished with Debbie McCarren, she had come back into my life, only to push me away again. By the time I walked back into the house I was clenched tight with anger and frustration.

In the half hour or so I'd been away, Johnny's fortunes had changed significantly. His chip pile was much lower, while Glen Van Dine's was much higher. It also seemed as if they'd exchanged playing strategies. Now Johnny sat impassively, his smile and banter both gone. And while Van Dine didn't keep up a nonstop commentary on the cards as Johnny usually did, he asked questions, very specific questions. And when I walked in he was asking them of Johnny.

"Did you know what a whore she was right away? I mean, she doesn't look like a fucking whore, so I could understand if you didn't get that."

Johnny said nothing. He just sipped from the bottle of Blue Lake at his side.

"She looks like a goddamn schoolteacher, don't you think?"

Johnny looked at his hole cards again. I'd never seen him do that once the cards were dealt.

"But Lester always said there was nothing she wouldn't do. I mean, nothing."

The bet was fifteen cents, and while I didn't know what Johnny had down, he was beat on the board. He called the bet.

"She'd suck cock. Hell, she loved to suck cock." Glen Van Dine raised a quarter.

Johnny tossed in a blue chip to call.

"She'd probably take it up the ass."

The last card was dealt down, and Van Dine, with a pair of tens showing, bet a quarter. "Hell, she'd probably take it up the ass while she's sucking cock."

Gary Krynicki folded, and Johnny called. Glen Van Dine turned over a third ten, and Johnny just shoved his cards away. The blotches on Johnny's cheeks had turned from their usual pink to white, as if he were the one who'd come in from the cold.

"Hey," I said to Glen Van Dine, "how come you know so much?"

He looked up at me for a long moment, then he turned back to the cards being dealt. And to the table Van Dine said, "Anybody sitting on a stool next to Lester at PeeWee's Bar was sure to get an earful about his piece of meat." He had a queen showing, and he opened the betting for a dime. Everyone called.

The fourth card came around, and this time Van Dine bet fifteen cents. Once again addressing no one in particular, he said, "I wish I would have been there the night Lester made her give a guy a hand job right there in the bar."

Another card was dealt, and this time Van Dine bet a quarter. "Yeah, three of them were sitting in a booth, and Lester had her sit next to this guy and jack him off while they just sat there drinking their beers."

The fifth card was dealt, and once again Van Dine threw a blue chip into the pot. While Otis Unwin and then Johnny were debating whether to fold, call, or raise, Van Dine said to Johnny, "Here's what I'm wondering. Do you and your old man take turns with her? Him one night and you the next? Or do you get her the same night? First he nails her and then you take your shot? Or maybe it's like I said before. She sucks you off while he rams it up her ass."

Otis Unwin folded. Johnny's fingers trembled slightly as he took a blue chip from his stack and tossed it into the pot.

I walked around the table until I stood behind Glen Van Dine. Before the next card was dealt, I kicked the back of Van Dine's chair hard enough to jolt him forward against the table. The ashtray at his side jumped and spilled out a load of ashes and cigarette butts. Gary Krynicki grabbed his wobbling beer bottle before it toppled to the floor.

Van Dine spun around. "What the fuck . . . ?"

"I liked you better when you were quiet," I said.

Van Dine surveyed the room as if he were trying to understand not only who I was, but also if I were part of an alliance that had been formed without his awareness.

I nodded in Johnny's direction. "I'm his friend, if that's what you're wondering. But he's too nice a guy to tell you what a fucking prick you are. So that's my job."

"Like a fucking bodyguard?" he asked with a laugh.

"That's pretty close. And now I'm the one who's telling you you don't know shit. Not about him. Not about his father. And not about her. So either shut the fuck up or cash in your chips and get out."

Glen Van Dine rose from his chair, but as he did so he

backed up, careful to put some distance between us. He was a college man, all right, with his penny loafers, corduroys, and blue oxford shirt rolled above his elbows. His blond hair was already thinning, and his front teeth were a little too prominent. But girls, I knew, found both him and his brother desirable properties.

"Let's just play some cards," pleaded Otis.

"Hey Matt," said Johnny, "it's okay."

"Yeah, Matt," said Van Dine, "it's okay."

"I changed my mind," I said. "You either walk out of here now, or I'll throw you out in the fucking snow."

One moment the young men in that small kitchen were arranged to play and watch a card game, and the next they were all standing, pushed back toward the wall in order to give the two combatants room. Only Gary Krynicki thought to pick up his chips and put them in his shirt pocket.

Glen Van Dine's smile altered slightly. "I didn't think it was up to you who stays and who goes."

"Wrong."

Van Dine glanced around the room, looking, no doubt, for allies. But even his younger brother had become a spectator. The room was quiet and still.

"If you guys bust anything," said Otis, "my ass will be grass."

Van Dine pointed at me. "Hey, tell him. I was sitting here playing cards when he starts in with this bullshit."

I had two to three inches and at least twenty pounds on Van Dine, but I didn't know what that difference would mean once we came to blows. He was four or five years older, and I was never sure exactly what advantages age conferred.

"Why don't you guys take this out to the garage?" Otis suggested.

"Okay by me," I said.

To get to the adjoining garage it was necessary to go down three steps, through a heavy door, and then down another step. As if they had been given an order to evacuate, the group headed that way in advance of Van Dine and me.

Johnny and I were the last two leaving the kitchen, and he grabbed my shoulder. "This is stupid, Matt. What the hell is this about, anyway? If you're doing this for me—"

I shrugged out of his grasp. "Better get out there if you want a good seat," I said.

"I can fight my own battles, you know."

What was I supposed to say to that? No, Johnny, you can't? This is my battle as much as it is yours? I didn't respond, and just kept walking toward the garage.

Starting in grade school, I'd developed a reputation as someone who wasn't afraid to mix it up, and over the years I'd had more than my share of scuffles and fistfights. But what others might have seen as aggression on my part was in truth closer to impatience. When it looked as though a fight was imminent, I almost always wanted to get right to it. This probably was another example of what Dr. Dunbar had called getting ahead of my skates, but somehow suspense was harder for me to handle than a punch in the jaw.

Glen Van Dine was standing by the open door to the garage, where cold air, concrete, and a group of bloodthirsty males waited. "What do you say?" he said. "This is your last chance to eat your next meal with your own teeth."

His line sounded scripted, and I guessed he was losing his enthusiasm for what was coming.

I thrust my middle finger in his face.

As I pushed past him, he threw a punch. The doorframe

restricted his swing, and as a result, he hit me with a clumsy, weak forearm on the side of the head, more of a clubbing push than a blow.

He drew back to hit me again, but I was close and quick enough to grab his arm before he could throw the punch. I pulled him toward me, and the two of us stumbled into the garage, scrabbling across the oil-spotted floor.

Still holding tight to his wrist, I gained some purchase and spun him around as if I were doing the hammer throw. I flung him as hard as I could in the direction of a wall hung with garden implements, and it occurred to me that he might grab one of them and use it as weapon. But when Glen Van Dine fell backward and landed hard on the concrete, the fight was instantly over.

His arm breaking sounded like an icicle being snapped off an awning.

Van Dine grabbed his left arm and instantly cradled it to his body. "Fuck!" he exclaimed. "Goddamn it! Fuck!"

Some of the boys in the garage had been Boy Scouts and would have known how to make splints or fashion slings, but it was Johnny and I who rushed forward to attend to Glen Van Dine and his injury. Van Dine continued with a string of softly whispered curses.

Johnny gently moved Van Dine's hand out of the way, so we could examine the injured arm. Johnny looked up at me and said the same word his father had spoken when he showed us the x-rays of Eugene Flint's broken leg. "Angulation."

Yes, indeed. It was not a compound fracture—the skin was not punctured—but the break was bad, and the displacement of bone had left Glen Van Dine's forearm looking like a roller coaster track.

Johnny reached into his pocket for his car keys and handed them to me. "You want to pull the car into the driveway? We have to take him to Dad."

## 10.

GLEN VAN DINE VOICED NO OBJECTION to Johnny and
me staying in the room while Dr. Dunbar assessed and
repaired his broken arm. In fact, from the way Glen kept
glaring at me I guessed he might have thought that my
having to watch would serve as punishment for what I'd
done to him. But when I did finally decide to leave the
clinic, neither guilt nor squeamishness had anything to
do with it. Quite the opposite. My anger at Glen Van
Dine was still running hot, but his injury had cheated me
of the satisfaction I would have taken in beating the shit
out of him.

I walked out of the clinic, but contrary to what I'd told
Johnny and the doctor, I didn't set out for home. Instead, I
wandered from room to room through the first floor of the
darkened Dunbar home, still energized by the adrenaline
that had fueled my fight with Glen Van Dine. On one of my
circuits I passed the wide central staircase. She's up there, I
thought. Up two flights and down a narrow hall, there was
her room. I could find my way there without a single light
to guide me. Would she wake when I stood in the doorway and whispered her name? Or did she sleep with the

door closed? Would she answer when I softly knocked? And when I told her what I had done that night, how I had broken a man's arm because he insulted her, would Louisa Lindahl take me into her bed in gratitude?

But of course I couldn't climb those stairs. Louisa Lindahl was sleeping in another man's home. I was blameless as long as I remained where I was, but I would be a trespasser if I were to climb to her floor.

So I kept circling, though my spirit was baying like a hound. *Come down, Louisa! Come down to me!*

A few years earlier, on one of the many occasions when I slept over at the Dunbars', I woke in the middle of the night and couldn't get back to sleep. Now, when this happened at home, in our house so small it seemed as if every corner could be touched by stretching out an arm, my wakefulness sometimes turned to fear, and I'd lie there nervously, listening hard to make certain that what I was hearing were natural creaks and sighs—the walls and joists settling themselves, the wind rattling a window frame— and not an intruder, as improbable as that was. The fact that I was the man of the house probably accounted for my anxiety. But that night at the Dunbars', fear didn't accompany my insomnia, and after a few minutes I got out of bed and left Johnny's bedroom to roam through the softly shadowed spaces of that grand house. As long as I stayed out of the rooms where Dr. and Mrs. Dunbar or the twins slept, I had the house to myself.

It was a winter night, and the falling snow made it feel as if the house and I were adrift together on a vast, calm sea. Mrs. Dunbar had left on a few low-wattage lights—a small table lamp in the living room, a sconce in the dining room, a tiny bulb in a candlestick type of fixture on the telephone table—and that night these lights seemed there for no purpose other than to light my way from room to room. I went from window to window, parting the heavy brocade curtains in order to look out, and while I couldn't see another light that had human activity as its source, every snowflake seemed to find some source of illumination in its descent.

Eventually I settled in a parlor on the main floor, where earlier the entire family—the Dunbar family plus Matthew Garth, that is—had gathered before a small fireplace to take in the doctor's stories of how deep the snows of his childhood had drifted, and how far into spring the lakes and rivers remained locked in ice. With the room to myself that night, I sat in the big overstuffed armchair that the doctor had occupied, and tried to situate myself in the chair such that my boy's body could feel and fill the indentations Dr. Dunbar's weight had made in the cushions.

I remained in that parlor for a long time, listening to the Dunbar house's sounds—less familiar to me than my own, yet none in the least frightening. I wasn't hungry and I wasn't thirsty. I wasn't cold or tired. I wanted nothing, and I wanted for nothing. . . .

Eventually I went back up to Johnny's room and the twin bed waiting for me. No one ever knew of my nocturnal prowl. My body's warmth would have left that chair long before the next person sat in it. But I was there nonetheless.

And so this night, when I finally turned away from the staircase leading up to Louisa Lindahl's bedroom, I wandered back to that same parlor. I sank into that same chair, exactly where Dr. Dunbar had been sitting in his robe and pajamas when we'd walked into the house with the injured Glen Van Dine. The book he'd been reading rested on the table, next to his ashtray and his Chesterfields. The embers of the fire that had warmed the doctor's slippered feet glowed faintly. While I watched, the nub of a log burned through and broke in half, spraying sparks harmlessly onto the blackened bricks.

But what if a spark should fly too far and land on the rug nearby, I thought? Smoldering there unnoticed, it would soon flare into flame. Then the house would be ablaze, and everyone inside would have to flee. Louisa would run from the burning mansion . . . into my rescuing arms. Try as I might, however, I couldn't imagine the realization of this fantasy. Not least, I suppose, because it would have necessitated the destruction of the building that I loved more than any other, and in which I felt more at ease than in my own home.

Frustrated, confused, and precariously balanced between incompatible impulses, I fell asleep in the doctor's chair.

Just as I had on the night my father died, I woke to the sound of Dr. Dunbar saying my name as he shook me awake.

"Matthew? It's almost three o'clock. Would you like to go upstairs and lie down in Johnny's room?"

Dr. Dunbar stood over me, smoking one of the Chesterfields from the package on the table. He was still in his pajamas, but over them he wore the white lab coat he always changed into upon entering the clinic.

I sat up straight and tried to focus. In the fireplace

there were only ashes. The parlor's chill was palpable. But I had barely registered the lack of heat when, as if it could discern my needs, the furnace clicked on with its customary thunk and sigh.

I looked past the doctor. "Where's . . . ?"

"Johnny went up to bed a while ago. Glen's in the clinic. The heat lamp is drying the plaster of his cast. He's in and out of sleep. He wanted to go home, but I insisted he stay here for the night. That was a nasty dislocation fracture. The ulna and the radius."

He sat down on the footstool. "Does your mother know where you are?"

I nodded. It wasn't a lie. If she looked in my room and saw I wasn't in my bed, she'd assume I was here. And that assumption was almost always right.

"Glen didn't slip on the ice, did he?" asked the doctor.

"He fell—"

"—Don't, Matt. Don't say it. Johnny told me what happened. Glen fell all right. With your help."

"I didn't mean for that to happen."

"Didn't you." The doctor turned and flipped his cigarette butt into the fireplace. "Johnny also told me what started the fight. I don't know whether I should thank you or spank you. But I have to say, I'm leaning toward the latter. What's gotten into you, Matt? The drinking, the brawling. This isn't the Matthew Garth I know."

What had gotten into me? Why, surely the doctor recognized the symptoms of Louisa Lindahl fever?

"Some of the things he said . . . He had no right."

"And now you've taken it upon yourself to determine what people have or haven't a right to say? That's awfully self-important, isn't it?"

He didn't expect answers to these questions.

"I'm capable," Dr. Dunbar went on, "of defending my-self against the Glen Van Dines of this world. And so is Miss Lindahl."

I couldn't help but notice that he hadn't included Johnny among those who could take care of themselves.

"But most of the time," he continued, "no defense is necessary. Stupid people say stupid things, and both the people and their words are generally ignored or quickly forgotten."

Dr. Dunbar was offering me a variation on the gentle-man's code of conduct, the same code Louisa had mocked. And in this case, I was with her. Far from being ignored, stupid things were usually remembered very well. And endlessly repeated.

He ducked his head down to look up into my eyes. "I'm not fond of having these talks, Matt. It hasn't been that long since the last one. Is any of what I'm saying sinking in? Do you understand what I'm saying to you?"

"I understand."

"And?"

"I understand."

He waited for more, but I had nothing else to say. The doctor flicked an invisible substance from the sleeve of his lab coat, then stood abruptly. "If you're going home, you better leave now. Your mother might worry." Dr. Dunbar turned his back to me, picked up a poker, and jabbed at the ashes of that dead fire.

The light snow that was falling earlier had stopped, but the temperature had kept on dropping. The packed snow

creaked with each step. And as I walked my irritation per-
sisted. It isn't fair, I thought, it isn't fair! I was walking home
in the cold while Glen Van Dine slept under the same roof
as Louisa Lindahl. It wasn't fair!

## 11.

JOHNNY PUNCHED THE AUTOMATIC TRANSMISSION button, shifting the car into neutral. Then he gunned the car's engine. At the stoplight next to us was a customized '49 Ford, into which its owner, Chuck Killion, had dropped a powerful non-stock engine. Chuck had also painted the Ford a red that at night looked like the color of blood.

Johnny put the car back in drive, and when the light turned green, he stomped on the accelerator. His father's Chrysler Imperial had 413 horses under the hood, but the car still hesitated a moment before the tires took hold on the winter-wet pavement. But within a block, we were doing fifty and picking up speed. Chuck's Ford was right beside us, so close that if he and I rolled down our windows, we could have shaken hands.

Up and down the street, car horns began to honk, the signal teenagers in our town gave to indicate a race was on. We were speeding east on Chippewa Avenue, four traffic lanes that paralleled the Northern Pacific tracks from one end of Willow Falls to the other. Chippewa was lined with stores, businesses, and eateries, and the glow of their neon signs doubled off their plate glass windows.

Because of its length, it was the street that the town's teenagers cruised to relieve their boredom. But after a few circuits, that activity could become boring, too. To make it less so, impromptu drag races broke out, taunts and threats were tossed from car to car, girls were beseeched to leave their cars and climb into others, and everyone was importuned for information about the location of parties.

This was a scene similar to those depicted countless times in movies and television, to be sure, but while Chuck Killion's car was right for its part, no filmmaker in his right mind would have cast the doctor's car—black, sleek, finned, and as long as a limousine—in this role. And in spite of the power of the Chrysler's engine, Johnny Dunbar never raced on Chippewa Avenue. He was a cautious, responsible driver, and he was also critical—we both were—of our contemporaries who lived to hear their engines roar and their tires squeal. As it was, I knew more about horsepower, cubic inches, and carburetors than I'd ever cared to learn, but the simple fact of the matter was that in our town, knowing which boys had the hottest cars was as natural as knowing who the best-looking girls were, or how the Willow Falls Warriors had fared recently.

Yet there we were, Johnny gripping the steering wheel tight while the Chrysler approached the traffic signal at the Sixth Street intersection with the speedometer's needle inching over fifty. The light turned yellow, but neither Johnny nor Chuck slowed. Yellow flashed to red, and only then did Johnny and Chuck Killion hit their brakes. The Chrysler dipped and swayed and its brakes squealed, but we finally slid to a stop.

"Okay," I said. "That was interesting. Though I don't know what the fucking point was."

Johnny didn't answer. To our right was Sandor's Mobil, much favored by the town's young drivers because gas there was always slightly cheaper than at any other station. Off to our left was Giff's Drive-In, where many of the town's teenagers docked when they ran out of gas money or tired of driving Chippewa Avenue.

Ordinarily we would have surveyed the lot at Giff's, looking for familiar faces or cars. But this time Johnny just stared straight ahead down the avenue's length, his hands clamped to the steering wheel. Next to us, Chuck Killion revved the Ford's engine. "We're not finished?" I asked Johnny.

He didn't answer. The light turned green, and Chuck Killion jumped away from the intersection, having an advantage because of his Ford's floor-mounted four-speed. But Johnny pushed the gas pedal to the floor, and the Chrysler quickly closed the gap.

We passed Bonnie O'Brien, driving her parents' Chevrolet station wagon, the vehicle full of our female classmates. We sped past Billy Woodyard in his black Volkswagen, and he bleated his horn as we went by. He probably didn't even know who was in the Chrysler.

We raced through the town's last traffic light doing fifty. Johnny passed an old humpbacked Hudson driven by an elderly man who was so startled by the black-as-night Chrysler flashing past that he almost swerved off the road.

The last of Willow Falls' businesses was on the right—Kendall's Automotive Supply, with its black stacks of traded-in tires behind a high chain-link fence. It was the last business within the city limits. And it was here that Chippewa Avenue became a country road.

The Ford was in the lead until Chuck Killion suddenly slowed, his engine growling as he geared down. In the meantime, Johnny was going over sixty on a street with a thirty-five mile-per-hour speed limit.

"Why don't you count this as a win," I said, "and slow the fuck down."

But Johnny didn't let up on the gas, and having left the last of the streetlights behind at Kendall's, we sped on into the darkness. Tree trunks and fence posts close to the road, black against the snow, flashed by like iron bars. The road ran ruler-straight for a stretch, before curving south and crossing the railroad tracks. I gripped the armrest tightly, but Johnny kept the Chrysler under control through the curve. Had a train been coming he wouldn't have been able to do a damn thing to avoid a collision. As it was, we bumped over the rails with a jolt that rattled my teeth.

We'd traveled about a mile out of Willow Falls. I knew this because I recognized a set of familiar lights and structures up ahead. If Johnny didn't turn, we'd enter the parking lot of Northland Screens.

The town's only industry, Northland was a manufacturer of door and window screens. The factory had once run shifts around the clock, but the business had been in decline for a decade, and of its reduced number of employees, none stayed past six o'clock. And so Northland's lot was completely deserted when Johnny roared across its blacktop. Then, for no reason I could discern, he hit the brakes and cranked the Chrysler's steering wheel hard to the left. The tires screamed against the asphalt. The car slid sideways, and if the surface had not been perfectly flat, we likely would have flipped over. "Shit," Johnny muttered softly.

My father and I had not been close, and among the reasons was his employment at Northland. He fitted screens to wooden frames—his endlessly repeated joke was, "lucky I didn't strain myself today"—on the four-to-midnight shift, so he was asleep when I got up in the morning, off to work when I returned from school, and there throughout the evening. Even on the weekends he was often with his buddies from Northland. Hunting or fishing were their announced activities, but according to my mother, those were simply excuses to drink beer and tear around the countryside. Somehow my diminishing memories of my father had matched Northland's shrinking fortunes over the years.

But I thought of him now for only an instant, just before the car finally stopped so close to a loading dock that I could see the splinters in its wood and the rust on its steel frame. The factory's windows reflected the night blankly. Then I leaned across the seat and punched Johnny hard in the shoulder.

"Asshole," I said.

Johnny slumped against his door, exhausted but elated. "What—you're the only one who can act like a crazy reckless bastard?"

"You could've gotten me killed."

"I thought of that. At one point I felt like I was sitting

in the backseat watching what I was doing. Anyway, we probably wouldn't have died. I mean, if we got into an accident."

"We probably wouldn't have died? Jesus!"

"I wanted to see what it was like!"

"You wanted to see what what was like?"

"You know, to take a risk. To not give a shit. Like the way you must have felt when you walked out to the garage with Van Dine."

"I was just pissed. That's all."

Mercury-vapor lights mounted on the roofline of Northland Screens shone into the car, turning Johnny's face a green so pale it was almost white. The ruddy blotches on his cheeks showed up as shadows. But the spectral light was a lie; he had never looked so alive. "Man, I wanted to stop so damn bad," he said. "So I just kept making myself go, go, go."

"That should tell you something. People who do this stuff don't have to make themselves go. They have to make themselves stop."

"Yeah, well, I couldn't have done this with the Valiant. Six cylinders sort of makes the decision for you."

I didn't remind him that cars were hardly the only means available for risky behavior.

"Hey, I forgot to tell you," he said. "Louisa asked if we want her to buy beer again."

"Why?" I asked. "Is she running short on cash?"

"I don't know why that bothered you so much. Rick Rizner charged us a couple times."

"I guess I wanted her to do it out of the goodness of her heart. So what did you tell her?"

"That I'd ask you. But that probably we did."

"And does she want to help us drink the beer again?"

"I think so. She gets pretty bored sitting around the house."

"How about this Saturday night?" I suggested.

"Why not Friday?" countered Johnny.

"Because I think I can get out of work on Saturday, but not Friday. They're having a big goddamn banquet. A fiftieth wedding anniversary or something."

Johnny nodded. "Mr. and Mrs. Angleton. I heard my folks talking about it. Dad said it better be a quiet celebration or Mr. Angleton is likely to keel over from a heart attack. But Mrs. Angleton, he said, looks like she could go fifty more with a new husband."

"If Louisa wants to come with us," I said, "we should find someplace to go. Someplace other than the car, I mean." My mother would be working Saturday night, but I didn't mention our place as a possibility. Although I believed Louisa's origins and ambitions brought her closer to me than to Johnny, I didn't want her to see where I lived.

"You didn't like my choice last time? Too many memories of parking there with Debbie?"

"We should go someplace where she would be more comfortable. Where she'd relax." I might have broken Glen Van Dine's arm for his crude remarks about Louisa Lindahl, but that didn't mean I didn't believe them.

"I know just the place," said Johnny.

"Where?"

"You'll see. It'll be a surprise. For both of you." Johnny put the Chrysler in gear and accelerated slowly away from the loading dock.

"And I'd appreciate it if you'd keep it under fifty this time."

"Don't worry," Johnny said with a smile. "That was just a phase I was going through."

Northland's owner, Stanley Wine, still lived in Willow Falls. And every year he promised the town that the factory would soon increase production and add shifts again. But it never happened. And in this regard, too, the factory reminded me of my father. He had often told me about what we were going to do together—fish, hunt, bowl, what have you—and when I was young the fact that we never actually did any of these things only added luster to his promises. He'll teach me, I thought, and then I'll be able to cast a line to exactly where the biggest fish drifted. . . . And together we would, we would . . . But when it came right down to it, we never did any of those things.

Johnny wheeled the big car back onto the highway, leaving Northland Screens and its high brick walls, blind windows, and motionless assembly line where no fathers were working.

## 12.

I WAS NEEDED FOR THE BANQUET, all right. In fact, so many people showed up to celebrate the Angletons' anniversary that Phil Palmer could have hired an extra ten people that night and still been shorthanded. His biggest mistake was allowing guests to order off the menu rather than simply giving everyone a slab of prime rib or a few pieces of baked chicken. The cooks, waitresses, and busboys hustled to keep up, and only the bartender's speed and generous pours (on Mr. Palmer's orders) kept the guests from noticing, or at least complaining about, how long it was taking for their orders to be taken, their water glasses to be refilled, their meals to be delivered, or their tables to be cleared. The night was cold, but because Mr. Angleton's circulation was poor, the heat had to be turned up, and we were all sweating as if it were the Fourth of July.

By ten thirty everyone had been fed, and the help had cleared out of the dining area so the testimonials to the Angletons' long marriage could begin. The smells of cooked meat—steaks, chops, chicken, and fish—were replaced with the smoky odor of cigarettes, cigars, and pipe tobacco. The clink and scrape of knives, forks, and china plates fell silent. A podium and microphone were set up in a corner, and the various speakers trooped up, first to tell a few jokes about the miseries of married life and then to drone on about what inspiring examples the Angletons were.

By this time I'd hung up my apron and stuck my clip-on bow tie in my pocket. Another busboy and I were standing by the open kitchen door, cooling off and sneaking a smoke, when Phil Palmer burst in.

"Matthew, go help Mrs. Knurr with her husband. He's outside the men's room and he's hurt his back or something."

Phil Palmer was not an unreasonably demanding or bad-tempered employer, but it generally was wise to obey his orders—and immediately. I flicked my cigarette out into the snow and hurried off.

Mr. Knurr, a Willow Falls attorney, was right where Phil Palmer said he'd be, leaning against the wall outside the men's room. His wife Beverly was holding onto him, bracing her weight against him in an attempt to keep her husband from sliding to the floor.

"Mr. Palmer said you could use some help," I offered.

"You're Esther Garth's boy?" asked Mrs. Knurr.

I wondered briefly why my identity mattered under the circumstances. Her grasp on her husband's suit coat seemed so desperate, temporary, and uncertain that she was in no position to refuse any offer of assistance. "Yes ma'am."

Mr. Knurr raised his massive bald head to look in the direction of my voice. His small, close-set eyes briefly focused and then went blank again, as if a second was all he needed to determine that I was not worth the effort.

"My husband," said Mrs. Knurr, "has a chronic back condition. He can't predict when it will give out on him. Which is obviously what has happened."

A first grader could have discerned Norbert Knurr's true condition. He was so drunk he couldn't stand, much less walk. "Obviously," I replied.

"I need to get him to the car. And then home to bed."

Mr. Knurr was a large man, and I had doubts about our ability to transport him. I was about to suggest to Mrs. Knurr that I recruit the help of another busboy when she said, "If you'll grab hold of him on the other side, I believe we can manage."

And manage we did. Mr. Knurr gave no sign of knowing what was happening, yet somehow he was able to help us help him. While Mrs. Knurr and I supported his weight, he took quick little steps, almost as if he were on wheels, and the three of us exited Palmer's and moved rapidly across the parking lot to the Knurrs' black Lincoln Continental. We folded him into the backseat, and I made sure none of Mr. Knurr's appendages were sticking out before slamming the Lincoln's heavy door.

"Can you watch him for a moment," Mrs. Knurr asked, "while I go back for our coats?"

I assented, then shivered in my shirtsleeves while she went back into Palmer's.

She returned shortly, wearing her fur coat and carrying Mr. Knurr's topcoat over her arm. She held out the keys to the Lincoln. "Do you mind driving?"

"I'm still on the job," I said. "I should go back in."

"I spoke to Mr. Palmer. He knows you're assisting me." She jingled the keys. "Please? I won't be able to get him into the house without help."

I took the keys and opened the passenger door for her.

As I drove out of the parking lot of Palmer's Supper Club, I had a new understanding of Johnny's impromptu race with Chuck Killion. Like the Chrysler, the Lincoln floated so effortlessly over the streets that you felt there was nothing you couldn't ask of a big car like that. Even the risks I had accused Johnny of taking seemed reduced once I was steering one of those boats myself. Looking out over the Lincoln's hood was like looking across a football field, and it felt as if nothing could harm us once the heavy doors had thunked shut. At the first stoplight, I actually thought the engine had died, so softly did it thrum.

When the light turned green, I resisted the temptation to press hard on the gas and instead accelerated slowly across the intersection. Mrs. Knurr pushed in the cigarette lighter, and when it popped out, she lit a Marlboro. She inhaled so deeply and exhaled with such force that smoke billowed across the windshield. For a moment, the smell of cigarette smoke displaced the smell of Mrs. Knurr's perfume, Mr. Knurr's cigars, and the bourbon that both of them drank.

"You're the young man who's been working with Dr. Dunbar, isn't that right?"

"Dr. Dunbar has been teaching me some medicine."

"Are you hoping to make medicine your career?"

"Yes ma'am."

"I thought so. That's why I asked for you. With Norbert's

back being the way it is, I wanted someone who wasn't going to treat him like a sack of potatoes."

Right on cue, Mr. Knurr moaned from the backseat.

I asked Mrs. Knurr, "Do you think we should take him to Dr. Dunbar?"

"For now let's just get him to bed. If that's not the answer, then we can take other steps." She turned the heater up. "You must be freezing in that thin shirt. Do you want Norbert's coat?"

"I'm okay."

The Knurrs lived in a rambling brick ranch house in Rocky Run Acres, an expensive new housing development on Willow Falls' west side. Before the houses went up, my friends and I would bike out here in the summer, racing up and down the low tawny hills, confident that even if we lost our balance we wouldn't be hurt since any fall would only tumble us into the switchgrass, bluestem, and Indian grass growing in every direction. And in the winter we dragged our sleds out here and flew down the slopes without worrying about hitting a tree or boulder.

I drove up the Knurrs' long driveway and pulled the car into the garage alongside a powder blue Ford Falcon, the Lincoln's smaller mate and no doubt the car that Mrs. Knurr usually drove, like Mrs. Dunbar's Valiant.

Together we hauled Mr. Knurr from the backseat, but by now his wheels barely rolled. His eyes were still open, but he couldn't support his own weight. Mrs. Knurr and I half-carried, half-dragged him through the house, and when we finally got him into the bedroom we were both out of breath.

We laid him faceup on the bed, and I slipped off his wing tips while Mrs. Knurr loosened her husband's tie. I made a move to take off his suit coat, thinking I would proceed to his trousers, but Mrs. Knurr said, "Let's leave him. If I have to transport him to the doctor I don't want to have to dress him again."

"Dr. Dunbar makes house calls," I said defensively.

She smiled. "With all due respect to your Dr. Dunbar, I meant a back specialist. At a hospital." She motioned for us to leave the room. "But right now Norbert needs to sleep."

Throughout this conversation, Norbert said nothing and gave no sign that he comprehended any of what was happening. But his eyes, his tiny dark eyes, sunk deep in his piggy face, remained open. For the first time, I considered the possibility that it truly was his back and not bourbon that had him incapacitated.

On our way out of the room, I said, "Sciatica?"

Mrs. Knurr looked at me, puzzled. "Beg pardon?"

I was only trying to demonstrate my willingness to go along with the pretense. "Is that his back problem? Sciatica?"

"You've certainly been paying attention in class."

"Dr. Dunbar has been treating George Ginn for sciatica."

"You're not supposed to reveal that, are you? Isn't that part of the physician's oath?"

I felt myself blush.

"I'm only teasing you," said Mrs. Knurr. We were in the living room now, and she asked, "Do you mind staying for just a bit? If Norbert gets worse, I'll need your help moving him."

"Okay."

She switched on a lamp beside a brocade couch that

was longer than any I'd ever seen. She tossed her fur coat on one end of the couch, and I sat on the other. She was also wearing a short wool jacket, and she took that off as well.

"Can I get you something?" Mrs. Knurr asked. "A Coke? Or I could make some cocoa? For this cold winter night?"

"No, thanks."

For a long moment, Mrs. Knurr stood silently before me. In only slight ways was she dressed any differently from the other women at the banquet, but those differences were significant. Her strapless cocktail dress, a deep burgundy with a faintly iridescent sheen, was cut lower and tighter than any other woman's. And Mrs. Knurr had the kind of voluptuous figure very much in vogue at that time—the shape men mimed by carving an hourglass in the air. I couldn't imagine any other woman in Willow Falls displaying as much cleavage as Mrs. Knurr. In addition to her curvy body, she had a wide mouth, full lips, large dark eyes, and high cheekbones. She stood there before me, almost as if she were encouraging me to stare at her without interruption.

But I was a teenager, and she was in her forties. She had shoulder-length hair so black it had to be dyed. Her makeup was thickly applied—especially her lipstick, which was a bright crimson, while the girls my age were painting their lips pale that year. Her flesh, tanned even in winter, had begun to take on a leathery look. Her features were oddly flattened and misshapen, and her smile only put things further off-kilter. If the word "blowsy" had been part of my seventeen-year-old vocabulary, I would have attached it to Beverly Knurr.

Mrs. Knurr finally broke her pose, and if she'd stood

perfectly still while allowing me to look her over, now her steps were unsteady as she retrieved her purse from on top of a stereo housed in a coffin-sized mahogany cabinet. She lit another Marlboro, then held the pack out to me. "Cigarette?"

"No, thanks."

"Would you like a drink?"

"No."

She smiled. "I understand. How could you possibly answer yes to that question. But if you'll excuse me . . ."

She didn't leave me alone, not exactly. A covered cage in the corner of the living room gave off a tinny, tinkling rattle, evidence that the bird inside (a parakeet, probably) was alive and well. Graduation photos of the Knurr offspring stared soberly at me from a bookshelf. Marilyn, two years older than me, was attending Iowa State University. Richie, five years older, had drowned in northern Minnesota the summer after his senior year.

As I considered these family photos, I remembered the rumors that kept my mother and the other town gossips busy. Beverly Knurr had supposedly had affairs with Mr. Foster, the gym teacher at the junior high, with a garage mechanic from the Mobil Station, and with an office supplies salesman who came through Willow Falls once every three months. The reasons for this wanton behavior were variously attributed to her heritage—she was Italian, the only citizen of Willow Falls who could claim that ethnicity—grief over her son, and her drinking.

When she returned, Mrs. Knurr had a glass of whiskey in her hand. She sat down on the couch a cushion

away from me. Then, as if she knew what I'd been con-
templating in her absence, Mrs. Knurr asked, "Did you
know my son?"

I shook my head. "He was older. But I remember the
news about . . . what happened. How shocked everyone was."

Mrs. Knurr nodded with understanding. "Norb has
never really recovered. People talk about how boys need
their fathers, but fathers need their sons, too. So they can
pass on all their useless knowledge about fishing lures and
curveballs and carburetors. . . ."

This might have seemed an insensitive thing to say to
a boy who had lost his own father, but I wasn't offended.
Quite the contrary. I was flattered. Mrs. Knurr's remarks
had the effect of a shared intimacy. Only those of us closely
acquainted with loss understood how refreshing candor
on the subject could be.

"I suppose," she went on, "it's not unlike your situation
with Dr. Dunbar. I imagine he's assumed a fatherly role in
your life? And then he's passing on his medical wisdom to
you as well. And to his own son, of course. Well. If you ever
feel as though you'd prefer a legal education, you should
knock on Norb's door. I'm sure he'd be happy to bore you
for hours with all the ins and outs of a lawyer's work and
training."

"I'll keep that in mind."

"But what he'd really like is someone to play catch with.
Does throwing a ball back and forth mean as much to sons
as it does to fathers? If the activity has any appeal to you,
be sure to look up my husband. He has the mitts and the
ball waiting in the garage for just such an occasion." The

rim of her glass bore the imprint of her lips, stained from her fresh application of lipstick. She was careful always to drink from the same spot.

"I'm more fortunate. I have a daughter on whom I can impose the same lessons my mother forced on me. How to match shoes and accessories. How to curl eyelashes." Mrs. Knurr leaned forward and batted her eyes at me. "How to tell real pearls from fake." She put her thumb under her own necklace and raised it, seemingly for my inspection. But what she was really inviting me to examine were her breasts, further exposed when she leaned lower and closer to me.

For many reasons, I'm skeptical of the episodes in books, movies, and television programs that feature the seduction of young men by older women. First of all, an inexperienced young man is often as apprehensive about sex as he is eager for it. And would a frustrated woman want a lover whose ineptitude would only add to her frustration? Also, while a young man might have a physical appearance that makes him appealing to an older woman, the odds that a young man will see a much older woman as attractive are much slimmer. Cheerleaders are often models for a teenager's lust, and those pert bouncy bodies present a difficult standard for a woman in her forties to match. Troublesome as well are the maternal thoughts that often play a role, even if they are subconscious. And finally, with Mrs. Knurr and me, as is almost always the case in similar circumstances, there was the inevitable gap between signals sent and signals received. The power of human desire is matched only by our inability to express those desires, thus guaranteeing that neither comedy nor tragedy is ever in short supply.

In this situation, for example, even though I believed that Mrs. Knurr was coming on to me, I couldn't be completely sure. And to have acted on a hunch—even a good one—might have been disastrous. What if I would have responded to Mrs. Knurr's flirtation the way I thought she wanted me to, putting my hand on her knee, or kissing her, or cupping her breast, only to discover that I had misinterpreted the moment? It was one thing to slide my hand under Debbie McCarren's skirt and have it pushed away. But were the same rules in effect on the Knurrs' couch as in the backseat of Johnny Dunbar's car? What if there were consequences I couldn't foresee, consequences more lasting and severe than a slapped hand or a reprimand? Besides, I couldn't stop thinking of Mr. Knurr's open eyes.

Abruptly I asked, "Is your husband's pain in his lower back?"

"Is . . . what?"

"His pain. Is it in the lower back? On one side? Because that's a symptom of sciatica."

Mrs. Knurr smiled knowingly, as if she were perfectly aware that concern for her husband was not prompting my questions. "You don't say," she said. "You're certainly set on that diagnosis, aren't you?"

"And the pain usually goes down into the buttocks and then down the leg."

"The buttocks . . . Really." She let go of her necklace, but leaned in even closer. Something she did with her arms squeezed her breasts together, deepening her cleavage and pushing more flesh out of the top of her dress.

"And down the leg." I shifted my gaze deliberately, looking into the autumn darkness of her eyes.

And then suddenly Mrs. Knurr saw something in me or in herself. She sat up straight and wriggled slightly to adjust her clothing. She swung her legs off the couch. Only when her feet were flat on the floor and the moment had passed was I sure: *I could have fucked Mrs. Knurr.*

"I'm sorry," she said. "You probably didn't know it, but we just had a little test. You passed, and I failed."

*I'm sorry,* I wanted to reply. *I don't mean to insult you, but I've pledged myself to another woman. . . .* But even if I'd changed my mind, there was nothing I could do at that point. Pity is an even more powerful antiaphrodisiac than fear.

"Do you prefer Matthew," she asked, "or Matt?"

"Doesn't matter." For some reason I had a hard time getting the words out.

"My son was always Richie. Until he graduated. Then he wanted to be Richard."

"I remember him as Richie," I said. "When he was on the basketball team."

"Matthew . . . ," she began, but then thought better of it. She lit a cigarette, and when she turned back to me her smile had vanished. Now her expression was close to a grimace, as if it were she whose back had gone out.

For a moment or two she simply smoked, exhaling in my direction and regarding me so coolly I began to calculate how far it was from the Knurr house to my own, and what the effect would be of traveling that distance in the subzero cold without a coat, hat, or gloves. Although the surrounding hills were now dotted with houses, divided by pavement and leveled into lawns, the terrain was still mine, in the singular way that childhood play takes possession of place. I wouldn't walk, I decided; I'd run home and hope that activity would generate enough heat that I could cover the two and a half miles without freezing.

Then Mrs. Knurr smiled once more. Her face lifted unevenly and one eye squinted almost shut, yet she looked more beautiful, if sadly so, than she had when she was posing for me.

"Tell me," she said, "what else have you learned from Dr. Morgan? Oops. Dr. Dunbar. But that's what some women call him. You know, from the comic strip? Rex Morgan, Rex Dunbar. I've also heard 'Sexy Rexy.' You know, like Rex Harrison."

"He concentrates on teaching us about the most common problems. Because that's what a doctor is most likely to see. Besides, he says, the other stuff's for specialists."

"And now he has a new protégée, I understand? The young woman the Dunbars have taken in? Is he instructing her as well?"

"She's mostly making appointments. And doing some bookkeeping."

"How does Mrs. Dunbar feel about their houseguest? Although I can't imagine that little china doll complaining about much of anything. And the way she stares up at that husband of hers when they're out in public? I can't help it. All I can think is, does anyone fall for that act?"

My impulse was to protect Mrs. Dunbar, but I could only defend one woman at a time. "Mrs. Dunbar feels sorry for her. For Louisa Lindahl. She's had a hard life."

"I should say. Getting shot certainly qualifies in that regard."

"I meant before. But Lester Huston was crazy."

Mrs. Knurr exhaled a stream of smoke and innocently asked, "Before he met her or after?"

I knew what Mrs. Knurr was implying, but I had no answer for that question. "She came from a real poor family."

"I'm sure she did." She finished her drink in one long swallow, the ice cubes bumping against her teeth. "She strikes me as a bit of a plain Jane, but something about her must rile men up. I've pissed off a few men over the years, but none of them took a shot at me."

Mrs. Knurr bent over, but this time it was not an invitation to look down her dress. "Well," she said, slipping on her shoes, "I'd better get you back to Palmer's. Phil would probably like your help with cleaning up."

At Mrs. Knurr's insistence, I drove once again. Nothing but the big Lincoln was moving at that hour on the curving streets of Rocky Run Acres. The sprawling ranch houses, set far back from the street, were all dark and silent. The smell of Mrs. Knurr's perfume filled my nostrils and the smoke from her cigarette stung my eyes. And suddenly it occurred to me that this darkened housing development was a kind of adult equivalent of Frenchman's Forest, a place men and women built for themselves so they could smoke, drink, and conduct their sexual experiments away from judging eyes. When Mrs. Knurr offered me a cigarette, I accepted it and let her light it for me.

"Do you have a girlfriend?"

"Sort of."

"What does that mean?"

"She can't decide between me and another guy. I'm not exactly sure what to do." If my evening with the Knurrs had taught me nothing else, I'd learned that a falsehood could be stated without fear of contradiction—*my husband has injured his back*—and that others would pretend right along with you.

"The thing is," I gently added, "he's my friend."

Only three cars were still in the parking lot when we pulled in to Palmer's, but my mother's DeSoto was one of them. I pulled alongside it and got out. Mrs. Knurr slid over. She looked very comfortable behind the steering wheel of the Lincoln, and I wondered if the smaller car belonged to her husband.

"Thank you for your help tonight, Matthew. And don't forget—if you ever feel like throwing a ball around, Norb would welcome the company." Although euphemism and metaphor had been the rule that night, this remark was neither.

My mother was sitting at the bar, and Phil Palmer was with her, standing behind the bar. Phil was a buzz-cut, rock-jawed ex-Marine, and he believed his success as a restaurateur was attributable to his policy of giving a customer an occasional free drink or dessert. Some people said he kept a list in his office, so he never gave anything away to the same customer in the same year.

Both Phil and my mother were smoking, and they both had drinks in front of them. My mother's represented the only drinking she ever did: a single brandy old-fashioned at the end of her shift. Phil, on the other hand, drank from the time he arrived at his supper club early in the afternoon until he left early in the morning. He always drank beer, and never in front of the customers. All the staff knew that the open bottle of Budweiser on the counter just inside the kitchen door was Phil's, and that it was not to be disturbed, no matter how long it had been sitting there.

Phil asked me, "Did ya get Norbert tucked in?"

"He's down for the count."

He cocked his eyebrows. "How about the Missus? Get her tucked in, too?"

"She's still out and about."

"I bet she is. On the prowl is more like it. Hey, you want something to drink, Matt? A beer? A soda?" With a sweep of his arm he took in the array of bottles behind him, indicating that I could order anything I liked. "Something stronger?"

I looked at my mother, and she shrugged. I pointed to her glass. "Can I have one of those?"

"Like mother, like son," said Phil. "Coming right up."

I sat down on the stool next to my mother. She was leaning her head on her hand, looking tired enough to fall asleep at the bar. "So," my mother said, "you've done your good deed for the day."

Her pack of Pall Malls was on the bar. I took one and lit it. "Mrs. Knurr said if I have any interest in being a lawyer I should look up Mr. Knurr and he'll be glad to give me some advice."

"I thought you were headed toward the medical profession."

"Just trying to keep all the possibilities open."

"Well, lawyering pays well, too. Not as good as a doctor, but then lawyers don't have to put their hands right into the body's muck."

Phil put my drink down on the bar. "No fruit in yours,

Matt. That's all put away, and I'm not about to get it out just to make your drink look pretty."

My mother reached into her glass and grabbed the stem of the cherry. "Don't ever say I didn't make any sacrifices for you," she said, dropping the cherry into my glass. She was joking, but her tone allowed her to convey a truth she needed her son to know. I thanked her and took a swallow of the drink, which was sweet and bracing.

"You sure you don't want to work tomorrow night?" Phil asked. "It's supposed to be cold, and for some reason the cold brings out the customers."

"It's a Minnesotan's idea of a big adventure," my mother said, as if she hadn't lived in the state all her life.

"Sorry," I replied. "I've got a date."

"You sure? Tony went home sick tonight, so he probably won't be in. I'll pay you what I would've paid the both of you. In cash."

"Nope. Can't do it."

"Okay, Matt," said Phil, "I hope the cold's good for your business, too." He roared with laughter and slapped the bar.

I wasn't sure what he meant, but it was next to impossible not to laugh along with Phil Palmer.

Then, quite abruptly, my laughter stopped. Somehow I felt as if I were being wooed. *Sit down, Matt. Want a drink? Relax. Have a smoke. Join us.*

I finished my drink and crushed out my cigarette. "I'll go out and warm up the car," I said, heading for the door.

## 13.

WE WERE ALL STANDING in the Dunbars' kitchen, the doctor and his wife, Louisa, Johnny, and I. I was wearing loafers I had polished that afternoon. My gray flannel trousers were freshly pressed, and under the navy blue V-neck sweater was a white shirt and tie usually reserved for Sunday mornings. Louisa looked me over from head to toe and smiled.

"Where are you going again?" asked Mrs. Dunbar.

"To the show," replied Johnny, "and then over to the Johnsons' to watch *Shockerama.*" Johnny's lie was excellent. There were three Johnsons in our class, and we had already seen the Wolfman movie that would be shown that night.

Johnny was wearing jeans and a sweatshirt, and Louisa was in her usual outfit—the cotton print dress and oversize cardigan. They were both dressed for an evening that wasn't supposed to be anything special, but I couldn't help myself. Practicing a deception twice, as I had the previous evening with Mrs. Knurr and then with Phil Palmer and my mother, must have been sufficient for me to convince myself that I had a date with my girlfriend tonight.

Louisa needed no more than a single look at what I was wearing to know what my ambitions were. Then Dr. Dunbar, who must have been keeping a close watch on Louisa, noticed as well. He pinched his own shirt collar to call attention to my tie. "And you, Matt? Are you heading straight to church after?"

Johnny knew me well enough to realize that my embarrassment might get in the way of my ability to provide an answer, and so he replied, "He's trying to impress her parents."

"Oh," said Mrs. Dunbar, "then this is like a double date?"

At the mention of a date, the twins, who were eating ice cream at the kitchen table, looked up expectantly.

Mrs. Dunbar had tried to sound playful as she asked the question, but her frown revealed how she truly felt about the prospect of her son taking Louisa Lindahl out on a date. Dr. Dunbar looked none too pleased himself. Yet both Dunbars had encouraged Louisa to go out and socialize with people closer to her own age.

"More like we're the chaperones," joked Johnny. His parents looked relieved and the twins went back to their ice cream.

Johnny put on his coat, and Dr. Dunbar helped Louisa with hers. "Are you sure about going out in the company of these two troublemakers?" That, too, was supposed to be a joke, but I couldn't help but think that the doctor would have been happy if Louisa had changed her mind and decided to stay home and make popcorn.

"I'm sure I can keep these two in line." She laughed her mature, innocent laugh, meant to calm any fears.

Then, as soon as we were in the Valiant, I heard a more

conspiratorial laugh, as she slapped Johnny harmlessly on the arm. "What a liar! I'm impressed. Did you have those planned?"

"Totally spur of the moment!" Johnny said, with the same elation he had displayed after racing Chuck Killion on Chippewa Avenue.

Just as Phil Palmer had predicted, the night was cold—eight below according to the thermometer on the side of the Dunbars' garage—and every word we spoke was wrapped in vapor. On our way out of town we passed Palmer's Supper Club, and from the number of cars in the parking lot it looked as if Phil's other prediction had been borne out as well. I couldn't imagine how the cold would work to the advantage of my "business," as Phil had termed it. But I could hope.

"That's where you work, right?" Louisa asked me.

"Right."

"But not tonight? How come?"

"To be with you." Why was it that every time I said something to Louisa with the hope of impressing her it came out sounding as if it should have been spoken ironically? And the laugh it elicited sounded like pure mockery.

Johnny and I waited in the car while Louisa went into the Red Hawk Bar.

"Okay," I said. "Enough with the suspense. Where are we going?"

"I thought we'd drive out to Merchants." Merchants was a public golf course situated on the hills north of Willow Falls.

"How the hell is that any different from parking in Frenchman's Forest?"

"Think back. Last October? The key?"

I needed no more than that. One Saturday the previous fall, Dr. Dunbar, Mel Howell, Johnny, and I had played the season's final round of golf. The weather was wretched—wind, cold, and an occasional gust of sleet. We teed off late, and before we did, Ernie Russell, who owned the place, told us that if we needed to get back inside the clubhouse when we finished our round, we could use the key that was always kept in the hollow of an oak.

"What do you think?" asked Johnny. "The locker room?"

"It's not even heated."

"At least it's inside."

"Okay. I guess." Then I lowered my voice, though Louisa had not yet exited the bar. "Do you suppose you could do me a favor? If it looks like she's getting tight, could you make up a reason for leaving? Just for a while?"

"Where would I—"

"Come on. Give me a turn."

Johnny drew back, and while I knew him and his moods quite well, I wasn't sure whether he was bewildered or offended. "A turn? A turn at what?"

"You know, being alone with her."

"What the hell do you think the two of us have been doing anyway?"

"I have no idea. Since you haven't told me a goddamn thing."

"Because there's nothing to tell! Her bedroom is on the third floor. Mine's on the second. She sits across from me at dinner. We hardly see each other."

"And yet I keep hearing about the conversations the two of you have."

"Conversations? What conversations? What the hell are you talking about?"

I pulled off a glove and held my hand down by the heat vent in order to feel if the air was warming up. "You said the two of you were talking about school. . . ."

"I was doing homework, okay? And she asked which subject was hardest. She never finished high school, okay? She wants to know how it works."

"And you're willing to fill her in. . . ."

"Why the hell wouldn't I?"

"Is she like your big sister or something?"

"She's—"

"Go ahead—she's what?"

"She's . . . she's nothing. Nothing more than a woman who's living with us for a while."

"For how long?"

Johnny gripped the top of the steering wheel, leaned forward, and rested his head against his hands. "Jesus, Matt. Do you know how you sound?"

"Suppose you tell me."

"Like an asshole, all right? A real asshole."

"Gee. When even your best friend won't tell you."

He sat back up, but kept his grip on the steering wheel and his gaze on the Red Hawk. "Yeah, well. Maybe it's just a phase you're going through."

I pulled up my sleeve as if to look at my watch. She should have reappeared by now. "I wonder what's taking her so long."

Then Johnny asked, "Suppose I do leave you alone with her. Where the hell am I supposed to go, anyway?"

"Forget it. Sorry I asked."

We sat in silence, staring hopefully at the entrance of the Red Hawk Bar like a pair of dogs waiting for their owner to reappear.

A Ford station wagon pulled into the lot and parked near us. Its doors opened and Johnny said, "Get down, get *down*!"

I slumped in my seat, prepared to drop all the way to the floor if necessary.

"Mr. Veal," Johnny whispered. "And a woman."

Merlyn Veal was our algebra teacher, a tall, lanky, humorless young man a few years out of college. Mr. Veal was a demanding, difficult teacher, and it was rumored that his high standards had put his job in jeopardy. The high school principal, Mr. Linton, had supposedly reprimanded Mr. Veal for the many low grades he dispensed. A teacher was free to give as many Cs as he or she wished, and Ds and Fs could be assigned to the Darrell Knapps and Barbara Turchiks without concern—after all, even if they managed to graduate, they wouldn't be going any farther than Northland Screens—but when a teacher failed Mary Wynn, the daughter of the principal of Emerson Elementary School, or Bobby Karlstad, the son of the school board president, then that teacher had to be reined in.

I peered cautiously out the windshield. "They're going into the Red Hawk," I said.

"The woman with him—is she pregnant?" asked Johnny.

"Big as a house."

Johnny sat up again. "That's Mrs. Veal. Dad thinks she's going to have twins."

"Why the hell would they drive out here just to go to a bar?"

"Think about it. How often have you seen a teacher go into a bar in Willow Falls?"

"Well, I don't sit around keeping watch at the entrances to bars."

"You'd want to watch the back doors, anyway," Johnny said. "Plenty of teachers won't let themselves be seen going in or out of a bar. Mr. Gregory"—Barney Gregory coached high school football and track, and taught world history—"will only go in or out of a bar through the back door."

"But it's okay to be seen inside? Fucking hypocrites." If the adolescent mind delights in any abstraction, it's recognizing hypocrisy in the world. And even though it exists in such abundance that not seeing it would require real effort, somehow its discovery always felt like real insight to us. And then it helped justify our own rude or lawless behavior—after all, *who were they to judge us?*

"What the hell do you suppose Mr. and Mrs. Veal do at the Red Hawk?" Johnny asked. "Sit at the bar and chug beers all night? Play pinball?"

"Nope. With that stomach she couldn't get close enough to the machine to work the flippers."

"You wonder why don't they just get a goddamn bottle and stay home."

"Because she nags him, I bet. 'You never take me anywhere.' When all he wants to do is stay home and work on algebra problems."

"She didn't get knocked up from him doing equilateral equations."

"I guess it's not a hell of a lot different from Louisa wanting to come out here to buy beer."

Johnny twisted around in his seat to look at me. "I've been thinking. Maybe we should have a signal or something. You know, for when I'm supposed to take off tonight. And how long do you want me to stay away?"

"No, man. I said forget it. It was a stupid idea, anyway. I shouldn't have brought it up. Like I'd ever have a chance with her."

Just then Louisa came out of the Red Hawk, toting a case of beer. And a paper bag. This time the beer was Budweiser.

"What took so long?" I asked.

She shrugged. "Just shooting the shit with the bartender. We're old friends now."

Smells traveled easily in the small warm cave of the car, and I could smell Louisa's breath. She'd had a drink in the Red Hawk. And it was probably on the house.

Johnny put the car in gear and began to back away from the bar. "What's in the bag?" he asked.

She reached into the bag, took out a bottle, and held it aloft. It was Regal House Red, a cheap sweet wine. "Lester used to mix beer and wine. 'Fucked-up juice,' he called it. Pardon my French."

"Literally mixed together?" I asked. "In the same container?"

"Sure. You open a beer, drink a little, then fill the can back up with wine. The more you drink, the more wine you pour in."

Johnny saw the advantage of this concoction right away. "Like an everlasting beer!" he said with delight.

"Exactly. Only stronger."

"But doesn't it taste like shit?" I asked.

Johnny and Louisa both groaned at my question, then laughed. It was the conspiratorial laugh again, and though I'd heard it often, it was never in chorus with my own laughter.

## 14.

THE MERCHANTS CLUBHOUSE SAT at the top of the highest hill in the county, and looked down on both the first and ninth holes. The ninth, a par five, climbed up from the valleys and flatlands below, so that golfers often finished their rounds panting with effort, especially in the summer. But the fairways and greens—sand until two years earlier—were covered with more than a foot of snow now.

Standing in this snow, Johnny, Louisa, and I huddled around a massive oak, keeping its trunk between us and the biting north wind. We were in the tree's shadow, as an almost-full moon slanted its light across the hilltop. Johnny groped inside a head-high hollow in the tree. "I know it's in here," he said.

"What makes you so sure?" I asked. "How do you know Ernie doesn't take the key out at the end of the season?"

"Because," Johnny said, reaching farther in, "I've got it!"

"Good thing the squirrels didn't beat you to it," said Louisa.

"Squirrels would have trouble carrying this off," replied Johnny, rapping against his gloved palm the six-inch length of lead pipe the key was wired to.

Snow had drifted against the clubhouse door, and Johnny and I kicked through its hard crust, clearing enough room to pull open the screen door. He took off his glove to turn the key in the lock, and we opened the door and stepped inside. "Don't turn on the light," I said.

"Why the hell not? Who's going to be out here?" It was true. The golf course was at the end of its own quarter-mile drive, and we'd seen no sign of other cars on the road nor out in the lot.

It proved to be a moot point anyway. When Johnny flipped the light switch, nothing happened. The power had been turned off for the season. Fortunately, enough moonlight found its way into the clubhouse for us to see, though dimly.

Louisa was right behind us with the bottle of wine.

No one in Willow Falls ever used the term "Merchants clubhouse" with irony or derision, but they might have. The dingy low-ceilinged cinder block building was longer than it was wide, and not much bigger than a trailer. Right inside the door was the counter where Ernie Russell took your money (unless you held a membership, as the Dunbar family did), and sold you a Milky Way and a Coke when you finished your round. Through a door was the men's locker room (women also golfed at Merchants, but they had no restroom or changing facility), which had a sink, a toilet in an open stall, a urinal, a single shower, and a row of ten freestanding lockers that had been salvaged from the old junior high school. In front of the lockers a bench was bolted to the floor. Even in the middle of winter, the clubhouse still had its characteristic smell of analgesic liniment and urinal cakes.

We went into the locker room, where I set the case of beer on the bench. Johnny was eager to try a wine-beer cocktail, and he had his own notion as to how it should be made. He opened a can of Budweiser and immediately poured half its contents down the shower drain. He refilled his can with wine. "We ought to have a funnel for this," he said. But amazingly, he spilled very little.

He took two long swallows. "Hey, this is my drink! I've never much cared for the taste of beer anyway." He licked wine from his fingers, then put his gloves back on.

Louisa didn't mix the two in a single container. She drank from the bottle of wine and then chased that with beer. She held the wine out to me.

"No, thanks."

"Wine on top beer, never fear," said Johnny.

"If you say so. I'll stick with beer."

Louisa pulled up the collar of her coat. "Christ, it's as cold in here as it was outside."

"At least we're out of the wind," I suggested.

"You remember how it was howling last fall?" Johnny asked me.

"I remember hitting a five iron into the wind, and it didn't go a hundred yards."

"It's like being inside a goddamn igloo," said Louisa.

I wondered again why Johnny felt this location was superior to his car, where we at least had a source of heat. This wasn't what I had in mind when I suggested that we find someplace other than the car to drink. Louisa was right. The locker room's whitewashed walls could have been blocks of ice.

As if he could read my mind, Johnny asked, "You want to go back out in the car? It's cramped, but there's heat."

It had more than heat. It was the car—and much of the drama, danger, and excitement of our lives occurred in cars. Johnny had been trying to please me when he came up with this location. But what was I thinking? Cars were the realm of possibility, and in them we had power. Things that could never happen anywhere else happened in the front or backseats of cars.

Louisa seemed to read my thoughts. "I'm getting a little old to be drinking beer in a parked car."

"Should we go back to Frenchman's Forest?" I offered. "I bet we could get into that place where you lived with Lester. Didn't it have a wood-burning stove?"

"I'm never going back there." Her tone was dismissive and resolute.

Always eager to lighten any situation, Johnny said, "If we keep moving, we'll stay warm!" As if to illustrate his theory, he did a few jumping jacks. Then he ran from one end of the locker room to the other. I don't know if all that activity really warmed him, but it accomplished his real purpose. By the time he finished his second sprint, Louisa was laughing.

"I lived for a while in this tiny apartment over a hardware store," she said. "The only heat was what came up from the store, and the owner would turn it way down when the store closed. Nights were so damn cold I swear to God I could have put milk on the kitchen table and it would have stayed as cold as in the icebox."

"Where was that?" I asked.

"A little town in North Dakota. You've never heard of it."

"Try me."

"Haugen. It's south of Fargo."

"You're right. I never heard of it. Is that where you're from?"

"My dad was from Haugen, so I ended up there a few times. There and on the family farm."

"And now you're going to live in Denver. Isn't that the plan?"

"That's right. Someday. And what's with the third degree?"

I lit a cigarette from the pack of Pall Malls I'd stolen from my mother's carton. "Just trying to get to know you a little better."

"Yeah? Why's that?"

"I think you and I have a lot in common."

Her laugh was like a stifled sneeze. She stepped close to me and scissored her fingers in front of my nose. "Here's something we have in common. I need a cigarette, too."

I struck a match to light her cigarette, and as she puffed it to life she cut her eyes up at me. It was the kind of look that sends you to the mirror to see what someone else has seen in your face.

Meanwhile, Johnny had opened another can of beer and was once again pouring part of it down the drain. This time it seemed as if wine made up more than half the drink.

"What did Lester call this again?" he asked Louisa.

"Fucked-up juice."

"That's a good name. A very good name. I can tell already this stuff will fuck a guy up. "

But the term that Johnny and I were likely to use was "tight," because it belonged more to the world of sophisticated adult consumption of alcohol than it did to the sloppy, stupid, beer-swilling behavior that characterized so much teenage drinking. And yet the word didn't really apply to Johnny very well. The more Johnny drank, the looser he got. His tongue flapped and his gestures became large, as if all his restraints were suddenly undone. I, on the other hand, could rightly be called "tight" when I drank. Because I didn't like to lose control, I always kept a close watch on myself.

Louisa followed Johnny's advice and moved around the clubhouse to keep warm. "So is this some kind of exclusive men's club? Am I in the inner sanctum or something?"

"Nah," said Johnny. "The public is welcome." He spread his arms wide. "The entire goddamn public. Give us your poor, your tired, your huddled masses looking to break par."

Louisa continued to explore the locker room, and in a corner, behind a mop and bucket, she found a furled banner. I knew what it said without seeing it unrolled: "Merchants Golf Tourney: Three Days, Five Flights." The banner hung over the clubhouse door every August.

But Louisa obviously wasn't interested in its message. She unrolled it only to drape it around her shoulders for warmth.

"Now that," Johnny said, "is how they should advertise the tournament."

Louisa struck a mock-seductive pose, as if she were wearing nothing under the banner. "Play golf with us," she purred. The line and the pose were supposed to be a joke, and Johnny and I both laughed. But Louisa's performance was so quick and sure that it also left me astonished. I had never seen her talent for mimicry before, and it was so impressive I realized in an instant that even if her talent was natural, it still must have been nurtured and developed with practice. I imagined Louisa in front of a mirror, imitating Edie Adams in her commercials for White Owl cigars. But then another thought occurred to me: Had I really never seen Louisa's talent for mimicry before? How could I be sure?

"Johnny's played in that tournament a few times," I said.

"Is that right?" Louisa sat down on the bench, using the banner as a shawl. "Are you a good golfer?"

"I'm not bad." Johnny took a long swallow from his beer can, then shook it next to his ear, as if hearing were the only way he could tell whether there was any liquid left. "But Matt, Matt hits the ball a mile."

"Not straight," I added.

"So who's the best golfer? Be honest."

"Johnny," I said. "By far."

"The best baseball player?"

"We're both pretty shitty," replied Johnny. He was already opening another beer and reaching for the wine.

"The fastest runner?" asked Louisa.

"Johnny. Not even a contest."

"The strongest?"

"Definitely Matt."

"I've seen the two of you studying your little heads off. Who's the best student?"

"That'd be Johnny. I don't think he's ever gotten anything but A's. Ever."

"I got a B in Latin," he said.

"But not for a semester grade." I finished my beer, set the

can on the floor, and kicked it across the room. It bounced and clattered across the linoleum, then came to rest in a urinal.

"Well, I know who the best hockey player is." And how, I wondered, did she know that? Had Dr. Dunbar somehow entered this competition? "Who's the best dancer?"

"Matt. He's had the most practice."

"With what's-her-name?" asked Louisa.

"Debbie," said Johnny, and reached again for the bottle of Regal House to pour more wine into his beer can. When he handed the bottle back to Louisa, she took two quick swallows, as if she knew that at the rate Johnny was going, the wine wouldn't last long.

"Here's one for you," she said. "Who's the best kisser?"

"How the hell would we know that?" I said. "We'd have to kiss the same girl, and then she'd have to tell us."

Johnny lifted his foot to rest it on the bench, but he missed and almost fell over. He giggled. "Or else we'd have to kiss each other!"

Louisa dropped her cigarette on the floor and crushed it with her foot. "Okay. Come over here. Both of you. Stand right here in front of me. Put your drinks down. We'll settle this now."

We arranged ourselves side by side in front of Louisa. She stood, letting her banner-shawl slip to the floor. Then she took off her gloves and put them in the pocket of her coat. "Let's see. Who wants to go first?" She squared her shoulders like an athlete before an event.

Without another word, she stepped up to Johnny, took his face in her hands, and kissed him on the mouth.

Whether it was the effects of the beer-wine combination, the force of Louisa's kiss, or both, Johnny lurched back a step when she kissed him. But somehow Louisa didn't lose contact. I wasn't sure if I wanted to watch them or stare straight ahead.

"Okay. Not bad. Some girls don't care how a guy kisses as long as he's good looking. But that's not me. If a guy can't kiss I don't want anything to do with him."

"How about Lester?" I asked. "How was he?"

"Oh, please." She put her hands to her ears. "Don't even mention his name." But then she brought her hands down and broke her own commandment. "He was pretty good. He wasn't the best-looking guy around, but he was a good kisser. He really was."

She beckoned me toward her, though we were only a couple feet apart. "Come on, come on. The contest isn't over. Next."

I stepped closer. Just as she had with Johnny, Louisa put her hands on my cheeks. Her hands were cold, but her lips were warm, and the wine she'd been drinking gave her breath a sweet mineral smell.

I put both arms around Louisa, pressing one hand on her back between her shoulder blades and cradling the back of her head with my other hand. But before I could exert much pressure, she broke away.

"All right, all right. That wasn't bad either. And I didn't get wet, rubbery lips from either of you. No runny noses. And no teeth in the way. So that's all to the good. But which was the best? Hmmm."

She pushed Johnny and me closer to each other, until our shoulders touched. "I'll need another round of testing." She popped her lips together a few times. "Once I get this settled, maybe I'll go over to the high school and write the results on a wall in the girls' bathroom."

This time I was first, and again I put my arms around Louisa and pulled her close. I felt her body's contours through the layers of our clothing. With this kiss her mouth opened wider, and her lips felt softer yet pressed harder . against mine. It seemed for a moment as if her breath was quickening, but before I could be sure, she pulled back.

"Next!" she said. "Come on, let's go. Quick, quick." Before Louisa and I had stepped far apart, she reached out and grabbed Johnny's arm, almost as if she wanted to drag him into our embrace. And as she did this, I resisted an impulse to push him away, to push him so hard he'd fall to the floor.

But just before Louisa could put her lips to Johnny's, he said, as if once again he could read my thoughts, "I have to go get my cigarettes." We were all standing so close that I felt the warmth of his breath on my cheek.

"Smoke Matt's," said Louisa.

Johnny was already moving toward the door. "Can't. Gotta be filters. Gotta be Winstons."

When the screen door slammed, Louisa said, "Jesus. What got into him?" She sat back down on the bench and reached for the bottle of wine.

The Valiant's engine grumbled, caught, then roared to life. As Johnny circled the parking lot on his way out, the beams from his headlights swept across the locker room walls.

"What the hell!" Louisa jumped up. "I thought he was getting cigarettes from the *car!*"

"He'll be back."

"He better be," said Louisa. "We'll freeze if we have to walk home from here."

"Trust me. He'll be back."

"Hell, we might freeze in here." She swiveled and sat sideways, bringing her feet up on the bench.

"You want my coat?"

"Aren't you the gentleman. No, I'll survive. You can give me another cigarette though."

I lit her cigarette and noticed her watching me again. This time her look seemed wary.

"Hey Louisa, can I ask you something?" Had I ever addressed her by name before? "What are you doing out here with"—I almost said "me"—"with us?"

She exhaled, and the plume of smoke had the same blue hue as the vapor of her breath. "Simple. I wanted to have a little fun. You know what it's like being cooped up in that clinic all day? All those tight-assed Norwegians coming in, and obviously they're sick or why would they be there, and when I ask them how they're doing, they say, 'Oh, pretty good,' because they think there's no sin worse than complaining. Or else there's nothing wrong with them and they come in bitching and moaning like they're dying. Shit, who wouldn't be ready for a drink after a few days of that?"

"Yeah. I guess."

"Now I got a question for you. I heard you've been trying to protect my reputation. By beating up guys. What put an idea like that in your head?"

So Johnny had told Louisa about Glen Van Dine's remarks, as well. "That's not exactly what happened. And it was just one guy."

"Yeah, well, don't bother. You won't salvage my reputation no matter how many arms or heads you bust."

"Why's that?" While we were talking, I was trying to think of a way to close the distance between us. Louisa Lindahl had kissed me—twice—and I had to make it happen again. If I sat on the bench facing her, her feet and legs would be between us. But if I sat on the other side, her back would be to me. I decided on the latter course of action.

"Why? You must be kidding. Because Lester and I were shacked up. Because he shot me, so people can't help but think I must have done something to deserve it. And besides, if the stories about me sound good, people will just keep repeating them. It won't matter if they're true."

Louisa's theory of how and why gossip spread struck me as closer to reality than Dr. Dunbar's.

"Are they true?" I couldn't have asked that if I'd been facing her.

"I can't answer that without knowing what people are saying, now can I?"

I swallowed hard. "That you'd do . . . anything that Lester Huston asked."

She laughed. "Well, you know that's not true. I already told you Lester took a shot at me because I wouldn't cook a Thanksgiving dinner for him!"

"You know what I mean. Anything . . . sexual."

I was sitting close enough to feel her shrug. "I guess. I can't think offhand of any outrageous request Lester made. But then he didn't have much of an imagination. Or much of a sex drive. Most of the time he was too drunk to get it up." She reached down to the floor, picked up the bottle of wine, and drank. "Is that the kind of information you're looking for, Matt?"

If I had been more sensitive to the ways people relate to one another, I would have realized how rare Louisa's candor about such matters was. But I was too intent on what wasn't happening to notice what was. "Is it true," I asked, "that you jacked a guy off in a bar because Lester told you to?"

"My, you have heard some tales, haven't you? You see, that's exactly what I mean. That story isn't true, but it really doesn't matter. It sounds good, so it gets repeated. And then it might as well be true anyway, because everyone believes it. And then of course it fits with what some people want to believe about me. And what really happened isn't nearly as interesting. Yeah, I grabbed a guy's cock, but not because Lester asked me to. Not exactly. I did it sort of on a dare. And because I was sick of listening to one more man's big talk. It was no big deal. Believe me, it was *no big deal.*" Her laughter then was painfully derisive.

I should have taken her laugh as a warning to abandon the topic, but I had come too far to stop now.

I swiveled around on the bench and put one leg on each side so I had better access to Louisa. I stroked her hair, then pushed down the collar of her coat and pulled the hair away from her neck. I leaned forward, but just as I was about to kiss her, she spoke up in a voice that was quite a bit louder, "What are you doing, Matt?"

I spoke into the warm hollow of her throat. "You did things with Lester Huston. Anything he wanted, you said. And you didn't even like him."

"Because I needed him. For a while." She lifted her shoulder, but only slightly. It was the tiniest of gestures, but there was no misunderstanding it. This was not the twitch of a woman excited by passion, but rather that of an animal trying to rid itself of a fly.

I sat up straight. "And you don't need me."

"That's right. I like you well enough, Matt. But I don't need you. You think you and I have something in common, but when I look at you, I just see another guy who wants to tear off a chunk of me. And you know what? I don't really need any more of your kind in my life. I don't mind putting out, but from now on I want it to be with someone who can do me some good. More than taking me out of a crummy little apartment just to move me to a crummy little shack."

I slid farther down the bench. "Is it Johnny? Is that who you need?"

"Oh, Matt! There is so much you don't get. Johnny Dunbar isn't interested in me. Not like that."

"Is it the doctor then?"

There was a long pause. Louisa put her feet firmly back down on the floor that was pocked and punctured from the spikes of hundreds of golfers. She stood up. "He'll come around," she said. "Now go out in that other room. I need to take a leak."

I walked out of the locker room and continued right out of the Merchants clubhouse.

The polished penny loafers that embarrassed me at the start of the evening now troubled me in another way. They were filling with snow, and I had barely started down the drive leading away from the golf course, trying to walk in the tire tracks of Johnny's car. The wind was quickly erasing them.

A subzero night like this one had a smell, sharp and

faintly antiseptic, and when I breathed it in my nostrils burned with cold. Somewhere far beyond this hilltop, grass grew and dirt sifted through the hand like flour. But much as I tried, it was impossible to imagine this in midwinter Minnesota. I had miles to go, my ears and feet already tingled with cold, and frostbite seemed a real possibility.

Out here everything was a shade of blue—the dark blue of the winter sky, the darker blue of tree trunks and fence posts, the pale blue of the snowfields. The moon had drifted south and risen higher, its light not much more helpful than a star's.

The road paralleled Harp Creek, which also served as a water hazard along the fifth hole. I'd driven any number of balls into it over the years. The creek was iced over now, and because I'd walked that terrain often, I could tell how impressively the snow had drifted along the fairway.

Perhaps it was all the cold and snow that caused me to think, when I saw the white Valiant in the distance, that it was just another snowbank, mounded high by the wind alongside the road. But when I came closer and recognized the dark rectangles of its windows, I ran, or as close as I could come to a run without slipping on the packed snow or out of my shoes.

The car's lights and engine were off. Two of its tires were on the road, and two on the shoulder. Johnny was folded over the steering wheel, passed out or simply sleeping on his own crossed arms. I rapped repeatedly on the window, and eventually he came around. He didn't seem the least bit surprised to see me.

He rolled down the window. "Matt. How long . . . did you . . . you know? With Louisa?"

"What the hell are you doing here? Are you okay?"

"I started to drive, but I knew . . . I couldn't. . . . I was fucked up. Like Lester said. Too fucked up. I was going to give you two hours and then—" He looked past me, or tried to, but his eyes wouldn't focus. "Where's Louisa?"

I opened the door. "Scoot over. She's back at the clubhouse. Waiting for you to rescue her."

"What did you—?"

I got behind the wheel and started the car. "Not a goddamn thing. Unless you count making an ass out of myself. And how the hell did you get so drunk so fast, anyway?"

He slumped against the passenger door. "I told you. Fucked-up juice."

By the time I had the car turned around and drove back to the clubhouse, Johnny had passed out again. I loaded the remaining cans of Budweiser in the trunk, and Louisa climbed in the driver's side and slid across the seat, careful not to disturb Johnny. His slumber relieved us of the pressure of searching for something to say to each other.

I drove to my house, where I'd once again hide the beer in the garage. But before I sent them on their way, I whispered instructions to Louisa. "Sneak him into the house through the back door. Dr. Dunbar might still be up, but if he is, he'll be in the front parlor. So take Johnny up to his room by the back stairs. If anyone sees you, make like you don't know what happened. Tell them Johnny and I went off by ourselves. I don't give a shit. Go ahead and tell them I'm drunk, too."

After hiding the remaining cans of Budweiser under the tarp, I took two beers into my bedroom again. While I drank,

I relived the evening, concentrating on what had occurred and what it had to do with human intimacy. These were not sexual fantasies, however. Instead, I replayed the conversation I'd had with Louisa, realizing that it might have led to something rarer than sex—friendship, which could develop further as we discovered that we really did have something in common. But, I also relived how I'd sent away a friend and let him shiver in a parked car while I tried to exploit his housemate. Maybe I could have reached some understanding, some insight into my character, from this line of thinking, but just as I approached that point, another thought obliterated all others: *That second kiss—it wasn't an act, was it? It couldn't have been.*

## 15.

LIKE OTHER FAMILIES OF STANDING in Willow Falls, the Dunbars breakfasted at the Heritage House's restaurant after church services, and anyone who observed those Sunday morning gatherings might have fairly concluded that it was not the children, but rather the men, who were so restless they couldn't sit still. Carrying their coffee cups, smoking the cigarettes or cigars they had gone without for an hour, the husbands and fathers moved from table to table, gathering others in their band as they moved through the restaurant. Dr. Dunbar barely sat with his family long enough to place his breakfast order before he was on the move. Like a politician seeking votes, he walked the length and width of the room, stopping at a booth here, a table there, and moving the length of the counter like a boy with a stick along a picket fence.

*Has that antibiotic taken effect, Mrs. Richards?*

*The Wildcats might have won that game last night with a stouter fourth-quarter defense.*

*George, are you and the Missus flying to Arizona this winter or driving?*

*That sounds like gout, Gary; you come in and see me first thing tomorrow morning.*

*No, Bob, I'm not ready to trade in the Chrysler yet, but when I am, you'll be the first to know.*

*Harold, when I hear a compliment like that I have to wonder if you've already started your campaign for state's attorney.*

*Jane, Tom, when I see the poise in that daughter of yours, I say to myself, now there are parents who did more than a few things right.*

*No, no, I don't think it's croup, Mrs. Ecklin. A cold, nothing worse. It's just settled in her chest.*

It was something to behold, Dr. Dunbar and the other men too, in motion and at rest, effortlessly ruling their town with nothing but small talk and handshakes. Their easy application of power remained mysterious to me, no matter how much I studied them Sunday after Sunday.

My mother had no religion, at least none I was aware of, yet when it came to her son she must have felt she had to take extra precautions to protect my soul, should I actually have one. She saw to it that I attended church, Sunday school, and confirmation classes. By then the habit was formed, and I continued to attend church more or less regularly. I was a Presbyterian for no reason other than that the Dunbars were, and the Sunday morning breakfasts at the Heritage House, to which I had a standing invitation, had as much to do with my church attendance as did any religious convictions.

Every Sunday I gave the waitress the same order: orange juice, scrambled eggs, a side order of ham, hash brown potatoes, a cinnamon roll, and coffee with cream and sugar.

And each time I placed my order, Dr. Dunbar followed it by remarking, "Is that all for you, Matt, or will you be sharing it with the battalion?" It was my favorite meal, but more than the food, I loved sitting at the Dunbar table on Sunday mornings, letting everyone see me there.

Since becoming part of the Dunbar household, Louisa had also been attending First Presbyterian Church with the family, which meant she also joined us on Sunday mornings at the Heritage House. She sat so quietly at the table that anyone who'd heard rumors of her previous wild life would have had to reassess them in light of this demure, respectable presence. Oatmeal, she would order; oatmeal and tea. It was exactly what Mrs. Dunbar ordered.

On the February morning after our night drinking at Merchants clubhouse, I watched Louisa for some indication that whatever she felt for me before had changed. But I didn't see a single sign, unless you counted the faintest of smiles that crossed her face when Johnny said he wasn't hungry and ordered only coffee.

The twins were trying to persuade Louisa to judge a contest they were having over who had made the best bookmark of a Bible verse that morning in Sunday school. Louisa ignored them until Julia stood up, walked behind Louisa, and tilted her head down so she had to see the strips of cardboard the twins had placed in front of her. "Which one?" Julia demanded. Louisa hastily pointed to one of the bookmarks, and even though her judgment was halfhearted, Julia whooped in triumph. Had I been inclined to give Louisa a word of advice at that moment, I would have told her not to be so obvious in her observation of Dr. Dunbar, and to pay attention to his daughters as well. But I didn't say a thing, and not surprisingly, Janet did not take Louisa's judgment gracefully. She glared at Louisa, to which Louisa seemed oblivious. Then Julia raised her first-place bookmark high overhead, waved it back and forth, and circled the table as if she were competing in the school carnival cakewalk. Janet slumped in her chair and sulked.

Meanwhile, the good doctor was part of a group—the wing tip, dark-suit, Vitalis crowd—who were gathered near the cash register, arguing over whether Willow Falls should build a new elementary school on the west end of town, in order to accommodate the population growth in that direction.

While the men settled nothing, Mrs. Dunbar looked nervously out the window. Snow had begun falling shortly after sunrise, increasing in intensity with each passing hour. Its descent now was nearly horizontal, and the wind blew so hard that the restaurant's plate glass window hummed and rattled in its frame. The street in front of the hotel was already drifted over in places, and it was clear that some of the cars parked on the west side of the street would have to be dug out.

"This is a blizzard," Mrs. Dunbar said more than once, "a real blizzard." Tornadoes in summer, blizzards in winter—Mrs. Dunbar had storm fear, an affliction not uncommon among residents of the Midwest.

As if he felt his wife's anxiety from across the room, Dr. Dunbar stepped away from the power brokers and returned to the table.

"I wonder if we should get going," said Mrs. Dunbar. She brought her napkin up from her lap and dropped it on the table, an action to be taken only at the end of a meal. Louisa did the same. The twins had stopped eating, and though I'd had more food in front of me than anyone, I was the first to finish.

Dr. Dunbar leaned toward the window as if he hadn't noticed earlier what was happening out there. "By God, it is coming down, isn't it?"

"We should get going," Mrs. Dunbar repeated.

"Right you are," said the doctor, and we all rose as if on command and began to put on our coats. Before we could move toward the door, however, Anna McDonough hurried over to our table. Anna was the wife of Dale McDonough, the owner of the hotel. They were a stylish and well-respected couple in their sixties, and they had both resided in Willow Falls their entire lives.

"Whoa, slow down, Anna," Dr. Dunbar said. "I have no intention of leaving without paying the bill." Although the doctor was making a joke, neither of the McDonoughs would have cared if Rex Dunbar never paid for a meal, so long as he continued to visit their establishment.

"Dale can't talk," she said breathlessly. She pointed to the far end of the dining room, where Mr. McDonough was sitting on a high stool, as he so often did, surveying the restaurant's operations. Like Phil Palmer, the McDonoughs were highly visible owners, doing everything from frying eggs in the kitchen to checking guests in and out of their hotel.

Still in a jocular mood, Dr. Dunbar said, "I'm sure Alice would like to hear how you managed that."

"No, I mean he's trying, but—" She was interrupted by a commotion across the room, and we all turned in time to see Dale McDonough topple from his stool and crash to the floor. While everyone in the restaurant stood to see what had happened, Dr. Dunbar took off at a sprint. Anna McDonough trailed behind him, her high heels clacking on the hotel floor.

Janet and Julia started to follow their father, but Mrs. Dunbar restrained them. "Sit," she said. "Whatever is going on, your assistance is not needed."

A ring of bystanders had quickly gathered around the fallen hotel owner, making it impossible to see what Mr. McDonough's condition was or how Dr. Dunbar was ministering to him. Earlier it had seemed as if Dr. Dunbar was among equals as he stood around with the other men, joking and discussing the issues of the day. But now those other men looked passive, weak, and ineffectual alongside the doctor, with his expertise and ability to act in the face of crisis.

While we waited for the doctor to make a diagnosis, I gauged the worsening of the storm by concentrating on the building across the street from the hotel. Frawley's Office Supplies had its name stenciled on the window in large black letters. Blowing snow whitened the words to gray, but when the wind gusted harder they faded away completely.

Fewer than ten minutes had passed before Dr. Dunbar returned to the table, his expression grave. "Dale has had a neurological episode." He spoke to his wife, but he made no effort to prevent the rest of us from hearing. "A severe stroke, probably. And his condition is worsening by the minute. Apparently he'd been complaining of headaches and dizziness recently, and just before he lost the power of speech, he said something about blurry vision. He's paralyzed on one side already, and has limited motor control on the other side. I can't do much for him. If he's going to have a chance, I have to get him to the hospital in Bellamy as soon as possible." Bellamy, Minnesota, was fifty miles to the northwest, and once the doctor left Willow Falls and its valley he'd find himself on open prairie for the duration of the trip, with barely a tree or foothill to block the wind.

Dr. Dunbar looked around the table, just as he had on Thanksgiving Day, after the deputy told him there'd been a shooting and he had to decide whether to join the search party or wait for the victim to be brought to him. The only difference was that now Louisa Lindahl was sitting with the family. And it was upon her that the doctor fixed his gaze. "I'm leaving right away. I hate like hell to ask this, but I need someone to ride along to monitor his condition. Louisa, would you be willing?"

It was all I could do not to jump to my feet and shout *No!* He couldn't ask someone else to do what Johnny and I had been trained to do! We were the doctor's boys—how could he forget that?

Louisa didn't say a word. But she stood immediately— the good soldier ready to do her duty. The only thing missing was a salute.

"Good. Thank you," said the doctor. "Alice, Mrs. McDonough will take you and the kids home. Louisa, you go over with Mr. McDonough and wait. I'll bring the car around to the back alley. Some of the men will help us get him out to the car."

Mrs. Dunbar reached a hand toward her husband, but stopped short of touching him. "But Rex . . . this storm."

The doctor bent toward his wife, his expression stern. "I have to do this, Alice. Do you understand? Dale's life depends on him getting to a hospital as soon as possible. I can't ask someone else to make that trip." Then the movie-star smile returned. "Besides, you know very well that this is the tail end of the storm. It wasn't even predicted."

"It will be worse out in the open. You know that."

His look hardened again. "I don't have a choice here, Alice. Don't make this harder."

Louisa had been edging away from the table during this exchange, and now the doctor looked her way and nodded, a signal so subtle that you had to wonder about other communications that might have passed between them without anyone noticing. Louisa hurried off toward Dale McDonough.

"With any luck at all," Dr. Dunbar said to his wife, "I'll be home before dark." But when he bent down for a farewell kiss, she offered her cheek rather than her lips.

The way the snow was swirling and billowing in clouds, it looked as if darkness might fall by noon.

## 16.

HOURS PASSED WITH NO LETUP in the storm, and no word from Dr. Dunbar and Louisa. Mrs. Dunbar chain-smoked and paced from room to room, looking out one window and then another as if the blizzard might show a milder face if examined from the south side of the house instead of the north. The twins worked on a jigsaw puzzle and quarreled ceaselessly about whether the other was deliberately hiding pieces. Johnny and I tried to study for a history test.

Of course, with the possible exception of the twins, we were all doing math computations. Bellamy was fifty miles away, an hour's drive at most in ideal conditions. But in this storm, Dr. Dunbar's travel time might double. That said, he still should have arrived by now. Even granting an extra hour to assist the doctors with Dale McDonough, we should have heard from him by now. Why, we all wondered, hadn't the phone rung? Or, for that matter, why weren't the doctor and Louisa home already?

For the third time that afternoon, Julia went to the telephone, dialed zero, and—though she was in a house full of clocks—asked the operator for the correct time.

"Stop calling," Mrs. Dunbar snapped at her daughter. "I don't want you tying up the line."

"It only takes a second," said Julia.

"Not even for a second!"

The wind whistled around the house's turrets and cornices, and the snow swept along the wide porch and hissed at the front door. Johnny's mother backed into the middle of the room as if she feared the walls might blow in. She put her palms to her ears. "This country!" she said, a comment to which she expected no response. I couldn't help but wonder whether Mrs. Dunbar was more worried about her husband being out in a blizzard, or that he was in the company of Louisa Lindahl.

I leaned across the dining room table and whispered to Johnny, "Let's go upstairs to Louisa's room."

Had I suggested that he and I take off our clothes and run out into the storm, Johnny could not have looked more dumbfounded. Nevertheless, he closed his history book and got up from the table. He didn't say anything until we had climbed the three flights of stairs and stood outside the closed door leading to Louisa's room.

Johnny put his hand on the doorknob, but didn't turn it. With his arm stretched across the doorway, he said softly, "Hey, Matt. What's going on with you anyway?"

"I thought this would be a good opportunity to have a look around."

"For what? What the hell do you expect to find?"

"Nothing in particular. But maybe something that would—"

"Would what?"

"I don't know." I tried to laugh, but it caught in my

throat. "Something that will let us in on her secrets and mysteries."

He twisted the knob and pushed the door open. "Jesus. You got it bad."

Louisa's room looked barely lived in. An iron-framed twin bed covered with a white chenille spread. A three drawer dresser that had a mirror attached to its back. A sagging, overstuffed chair that had once been in the Dunbars' parlor. A bedside table. A lamp with a tasseled shade. Lace doilies on the dresser, under the bedside lamp, and on the back of the chair. A framed reproduction of a woodland scene.

Johnny opened a curtain on a window facing north, and the light that entered the room was milky and soft. He stood at the window as if he were keeping watch.

I opened the closet. Louisa's canvas shoes and slippers were on the floor. Three cotton print dresses and that familiar oversize sweater hung from carefully spaced hangers. Her robe hung from a hook on the back of the door. A chipboard suitcase rested on an overhead shelf. Whatever I hoped to find wasn't in the closet.

I moved to the dresser and opened the top drawer. On one side were three pairs of white cotton underpants—I recognized the torn elastic waistband of the pair Louisa revealed when she lifted her dress in front of Johnny and me. One brassiere, its strap attached to the cup with a safety pin. I ran my fingertip around the inside of the cup, and my fingernail snagged on the fraying nylon.

Then I found it. There was a stenographic pad under a slip yellowed with age. I took the pad out and opened it to a page of writing I assumed to be Louisa's. On the top line of the very first page, written in pencil and in the hand of someone who pressed too hard and formed large, childlike letters, were the words, *Mrs. Dunbar.* On the lines below, in the same handwriting, was a list:

*Crosses ankles*
*Never chews gum*
*Favors Julia*
*Always leaves food on her plate. Never seconds.*
*Brushes hair first thing*
*Always wears heels*
*Never Kleenex, but always has handkerchief*
*Blots lipstick*
*Always uses cup and saucer*
*Never smokes cigarettes down to filter*
*Doesn't go out with her hair up*
*Doesn't curse or swear*
*Won't do what a man wants/likes—this is how I steal*
*him away!*

I scanned the remaining pages, but they were all blank. Johnny wouldn't want to know what was on that list, and I had to keep him from reading it. I replaced the pad and closed the drawer. Johnny continued to stare out at the storm.

"Okay," I said, backing away from the dresser. "Not much here."

"Did you find what you were looking for?"

"I told you. I don't even know what I was looking for. But I'd know it if I saw it."

Johnny shook his head in disgust and closed the curtains.

In truth, I'd discovered something far more exciting, far more intimate, than Louisa's undergarments. Her list reminded me of a folded sheet of notebook paper in the top drawer of my own dresser. On it, I'd printed my self-improvement list for the month of February: *Begin day with 50 pushups, 50 situps, 200 jumping jacks. End day with 3 rounds of shadow boxing. Memorize 5 Latin vocabulary words. No soft drinks. No cigarettes before noon. No chocolate.* How could she not see how much we had in common?

"Any other place in the house you'd like to snoop around?" Johnny asked. His tone was angry, and while I felt as if our friendship depended on my answer, that relationship wasn't especially important to me at the moment.

"Why? Do you know where the secrets are hidden?"

"What secrets?"

"I don't know, man. That's what makes them secrets."

Johnny shook his head again. "You're in sad shape, you know that?"

"And you sound like your old man. Is the lecture over?"

"Does it matter? You aren't listening to what I say anyway." We stared at each other across Louisa Lindahl's room.

We were on our way back downstairs when we heard Johnny's mother calling for him. She met us on the landing between the second and first floors.

"Take my car." She had the keys to the Valiant in her hand, and she thrust them at Johnny. "Go find your father." Before Johnny could question or protest, she turned and went back downstairs. "The snow's letting up," she said over her shoulder.

We both turned and looked out the window. If anything, the strength of the storm had increased. Snow crackled against the glass, and the massive elms bordering the Dunbars' property were nothing but shadows amid the swirling white.

"Mom," said Johnny, hurrying after his mother's fleeing form. "Wait . . . I don't think . . ."

She stopped at the front door, almost as if she were going to open it and stand exposed to the storm. One hand clutched at the open collar of her blouse, the other was clamped tight over her mouth.

"Did you try calling—?" Johnny asked.

"They left the hospital close to two hours ago. So keep your eyes open on the road, in case they're stuck in a ditch somewhere. Or in case you pass right by them."

"They left the hospital . . . ?"

"Did you hear me?" she said sharply. "That's my husband out there! If you can't do this for me . . ."

Johnny replied feebly. "It'll be dark soon—"

But before he could finish his protest Mrs. Dunbar interrupted, "So get going!" Her voice hit a pitch just this side of a scream, and Johnny clamped his jaw and walked away.

For a moment I considered taking up the argument on his behalf, but Mrs. Dunbar's half-wild look stopped me. Here was another item for Louisa's list: *Mrs. Dunbar will endanger her son in order to keep her husband from another woman's company.*

I caught up to Johnny as he was buckling his overshoes.

I started putting on my own boots. "Should we take a thermos of coffee?" I asked. "Maybe a couple apples or candy bars? That way we won't starve if we get stuck and have to wait out the storm. And we should take a few blankets, too. We don't want to freeze to death."

"What's this 'we' shit?"

"I thought I'd ride along. Just to criticize your driving."

"Don't be stupid. No sense both of us going out in a fucking blizzard."

"Sunday afternoon," I said. "I've got nothing better to do."

He stood, stamped his feet into his overshoes, and jammed his arms into his coat. He stared at me for a long moment. On the rare occasions when Johnny Dunbar was mad, his usually ruddy cheeks became blotched with white, as if anger pulled his flesh so tight that bone showed through. "Fine," he said. "It's your own fucking funeral."

"Then we should throw a shovel in the trunk."

He opened the door before I'd finished buttoning my coat. "Since when did you become the voice of reason?"

We stepped out into the storm. The snow on the porch was already three feet deep, and the top of the drift had been carved sharp by the wind. We hunched and turned our heads away from the icy sting of wind and snow. I shouted my reply to Johnny. "Weird, isn't it? It must be a new phase I'm going through."

## 17.

FOR A TIME IT LOOKED AS IF MRS. DUNBAR's prediction would prove to be correct. As Johnny drove us up out of the valley, the snow did seem to be diminishing. The air actually lightened, almost as if a window shade had been raised. The road was relatively clear, scoured free of snow by the same wind that had drifted over the streets of Willow Falls.

But then the road climbed and curved, and we were above and beyond the hills and trees that had temporarily sheltered us. On the prairie there was nothing to block the wind, and gusts rocked the car. The snow came at us in great swirling bursts.

Johnny clung determinedly to the steering wheel. The defroster worked hard, but was losing the battle with the multiplying frost stars that crept down the glass. The snow was of the drier variety, which allowed the wipers to keep the windshield clear.

There were no other cars on the highway, and this was a good thing, since the shoulder and center lines had been erased. Where the snow had succeeded in spilling out of the ditch, drifts crossed the road, and Johnny had no choice but to charge through them. The car hit them with a *whumpf,* and each time it did I expected the car to gasp and come to a halt.

We're not going to make it, I thought. And when our frozen bodies are finally discovered, would anyone think to attribute our deaths to the same cause as Lester Huston's?

Johnny must have had similar thoughts. We were barely ten miles out of Willow Falls when he leaned forward and hunched over the steering wheel. "I can't do this."

"Sure you can," I said. "Just keep your head down and plow ahead. One mile at a time. We'll get there."

"I'm pulling over. We can walk to a farm or something."

"What farm? I don't know about you, but I can't see across the road."

"We can come back for the car tomorrow. Or later today if this lets up."

"What about all those stories about farmers who got lost walking out to their own goddamn barn during a bliz-zard? No, man, you've got to keep going."

"I can't, Matt. I mean it."

"Slow down if you need to. But keep moving."

Johnny shifted his hands nervously on the wheel. "I'm pulling over. . . ."

"You can't. We might never get going again."

" . . . Then you can drive. I can't do this."

"Fine. But don't pull over too far."

Johnny found a spot where the wind had swept the side of the road clear for ten yards, and he eased the Valiant to the shoulder. When the car stopped it seemed less a consequence of Johnny's application of the brakes and more a loss of mechanical will, as if the vehicle itself had realized it was no match for nature's forces.

Johnny opened his door, jumped out as quickly as he could, and slammed the door. I slid over behind the steering wheel. For a brief moment I was alone in the car, and in that instant power and possibility and risk rushed through me. What if I put the car in gear and hit the gas, leaving Johnny snow-blind and freezing on the side of the road? The blizzard probably would have covered my tracks.

This fleeting feeling was strangely similar to something I'd experienced a few years earlier, when I was tramping around in Frenchman's Forest. On a late spring day I'd found myself in trouble in school for talking back to Mr. Gordon, who taught eighth-grade science. I'd been walking down the hall on my way to class when Morris McGill, a big stupid farm kid with a reputation for cheerful cruelty, stepped on my foot. He did it deliberately and for no good reason—he was next to me, I was wearing sneakers, and he was wearing boots. When Morris lifted his foot to repeat the act, I shoved him hard against a locker, and Mr. Gordon witnessed my retaliation. "You might have split his skull open," he said. Without thinking I replied, "A horse could kick him in the head and it wouldn't dent that skull." That was enough for Mr. Gordon. He marched me down to the principal's office, where he said, "Mr. Lucas knows how to deal with hoodlums like you." As it turned out, Mr. Lucas wasn't there that afternoon, but the secretary wrote out a summons (that was her term for the appointment slip) for me to return the following morning before school in order to speak with the principal. To make sure I didn't "forget" the meeting, she said she'd call my parents. Then I made matters worse by correcting her. "Parent," I said. "I'm down to one." Before she sent me on my way she told me she'd add smart aleck to the list of offenses to be reported to Mr. Lucas.

Rather than go directly home after school that day, I headed for Frenchman's Forest. There, I knew, I'd have an hour or two of solitude, time to calm down and to nurture the self-pity that so often trails in anger's wake.

I walked aimlessly, and because I was not determined to remain within the confines of the forest, I soon stepped into an open field. I stood at the bottom of a grassy hill. A few horses grazed nearby, but no owner was visible. Nor could I see a house, stable, or fence line. I wondered why those animals didn't leave. Why not head for the open prairie and its freedom?

I'd never been on a horse that wasn't saddled, but that didn't prevent me from briefly entertaining a fantasy of climbing bareback on one of those horses and galloping off. The thought was enough. Suddenly it was easier to do what I was going to do anyway: return home, tell my mother about my upcoming meeting with Mr. Lucas, and walk into his office the next morning.

As it turned out, Mr. Lucas wasn't particularly interested in me or my violation of school decorum, and he said little to me beyond, "Don't do something like this on school grounds." Which I took to mean that I could do anything I wanted to Morris off school grounds.

I gripped the steering wheel hard and turned my head to the side when Johnny opened the passenger door. Winter rushed in behind him.

"Jesus Christ!" he said, gasping as if he hadn't been out in open country, but underwater. "It's like getting shot with a BB gun!"

I wiped my hand through the snow that had dusted the dashboard in the seconds the door was open. "And above the waist is legal," I said. That was a reference to one of our youthful activities in Frenchman's Forest. Johnny and I and a few of our friends used to have BB gun fights in amongst the trees, and there was one clear rule: aiming above the waist was "illegal." In spite of our heavy denims, getting hit in the legs or butt could sting like hell and raise a welt. Still, that was our rule.

"You ready?" I asked Johnny, punching the transmission button for Drive. "Let's get this show on the road."

We were able to make progress through the snow-storm due to a number of factors. A recent summer road crew had painted a fresh center dividing line, and its dashes revealed themselves just often enough for me to be sure I was staying on the right side of the road. A farmer had strung his wire fence close enough to the road that the fence posts occasionally showed through the blowing snow. Another farmer had planted a shelterbelt of trees, presenting me with an extra fifty yards of vision. And then the telephone company's wires ran along the highway at intervals, and those creosote-coated poles were black enough to steer me away from the ditch.

Also, a driver, and I doubt there was more than one, who had driven that stretch of road before me, did so recently enough that I could sometimes see the faint impressions of his tire tracks, heartening proof not only that this highway could be traversed, but also that Johnny and I were not the only ones crazy, foolish, or duty-bound enough to be out in the storm.

And then finally, the wind that had blown so piti-lessly all day began to lose some of its energy and mal-ice, and gradually, gradually, after close to two hours on the road, I could see seventy-five, a hundred, two hundred yards ahead, so that by the time we were within five miles of Bellamy I increased our speed to fifty miles per hour, which was double what we'd been doing. At last the car's speedometer matched the urgency we'd been feeling since we drove away from the Dunbars'. As if our lightened spirits could affect nature, the western horizon began to brighten and the faintest blue pushed its way through the iron sky. The sun would soon set, but at least it wasn't lost to us for good.

"Looks like maybe the drive back will be easier," said Johnny. Those were the first words he spoke since I'd taken over the driving.

My hands had turned to claws on the steering wheel. I took one hand off the wheel and then the other, shaking each in turn and flexing my fingers. "Jesus, are you ready for another trip already?"

"I just meant . . . oh, shit. I don't know what I meant. What if we can't find them? We'll have to turn around and head back."

"We'll find them."

"We could've passed right by them and never seen them. If they slid off the road they could be in a ditch and—"

"—I said we'll find them."

And yet for all his worry and concern, once we caught sight of the doctor's car, Johnny wasn't ready to admit it.

One of the first businesses on the edge of Bellamy, right where the speed limit dropped to thirty-five, was the Wagon Wheel Motor Inn. For an instant the office and cabins—all painted white—looked like part of the snowy landscape. But neither the snow nor the frost sticking to its surface could have made that black Chrysler Imperial look like anything from the natural world.

Although the Wagon Wheel was on Johnny's side of the car and he was looking out in that direction, I was the one who exclaimed, "That's your dad's car!"

I slowed, but not in time to turn into the Wagon Wheel's lot.

Johnny, however, waved me on. "We have to check the hospital."

"But your dad's car is back there—"

"—the hospital."

I didn't have to look at him to know how his jaw was set. "What the hell? Is this because you know your dad and Louisa are there together? It doesn't mean. . . . They got caught in the blizzard too, for Chrissake." The thought of the two of them together in a motel room was as distressing to me as it was to Johnny, though it meant a different kind of loss to each of us. But nothing was to be gained by pretending that we hadn't seen the car.

"We're here to check on Mr. McDonough." Johnny was staring straight ahead now. "A stroke is nothing to fool around with."

"It's great that you're concerned about Mr. McDonough, but you know damn well that's not why your mom sent us here. She doesn't give a shit if Dale McDonough lives or dies."

"I think the hospital is on the north side of town. Up on a hill, if I remember."

The blizzard must not have hit as hard here, because the streets and sidewalks were clear in spots, and the

brick walls of buildings were not newly plastered in white.
Bellamy didn't feel like a town recently besieged. There
were cars on the streets, and in front of J. C. Penney's a man
was shoveling the sidewalk. Inside Lily's Café—featuring
Broasted Chicken to Go—a few patrons were waiting for
their Sunday dinners. Bellamy might have been Sunday-
evening quiet, but the straight lines and right angles of its
streets and intersections, to say nothing of its neon signs
and the headlights of its hurrying cars, were a striking
contrast to the prairie's whirling white chaos.

"I can smell that chicken," I said to Johnny.

"We'll get something to eat before we go back."

"Promise?"

"Okay. Yes. Hell, yes. I'll buy you a steak."

"I'll settle for chicken. That smells damn good."

He pointed toward an intersection with a Mobil station on one corner and a First National Bank branch on
the other. "Take a right up there."

"How come you know where the hospital is?" I asked.

"I was here to have my tonsils out."

"When the hell was this?"

"Fourth grade? No, fifth. Right after Christmas. Fifth
grade."

"Huh? How come I didn't know about this?"

"This might come as a surprise to you, Matt, but there's
a hell of a lot you don't know about the Dunbar family."

"Yeah? Like what?"

This was Johnny's chance. If he feared—or knew—that
something was going on between his father and Louisa
Lindahl, Johnny could unburden himself now.

He was quiet for so long that I almost expected him

to do just that. We drove down a block of older brick and stucco houses that looked as though they had been built by someone who knew how hard winds could blow off the prairie. Amber light streamed out of their windows, making squares on the fresh snow.

Finally Johnny said, "That I don't have tonsils."

## 18.

WHEN WE ARRIVED AT SAINT MICHAEL'S HOSPITAL, I told Johnny I'd wait in the car while he went in to find out if Mr. McDonough was a patient, and if so, what his condition was.

Johnny climbed out of the car, but then, before closing the door, he leaned back in to say, "You'll be here when I come out, won't you? You're not going back to that motel, are you?"

He knew me too well. Ever since we drove past the Wagon Wheel Motor Inn and saw the black car parked in its lot, I could think of little but the risks we'd taken that afternoon in order to find Dr. Dunbar and Louisa. And yet now, here we were, moving farther away from them.

"I'll be here," I reassured Johnny. "You're buying me dinner, remember?"

As soon as he was gone, I let my head fall back against the car seat. When I closed my eyes, I saw the snow falling again, blowing across a highway that buckled and waved in my fatigued imagination, as if the earth were heaving and shifting beneath the road's surface. Then another car emerged from that drowsy blizzard, speeding right at us in the wrong lane. I awakened with a jolt, momentarily surprised that I wasn't staring at the headlights of another car.

Fewer than fifteen minutes after he'd gone into the hospital, Johnny returned, running across the lot toward the car. He ran as if someone was after him, heedless of the parking lot's packed snow and ice. He stayed on his feet until he was almost at the car, then slipped and collapsed against the car to keep from falling. Johnny tumbled into the car and said breathlessly, "He's dead—Mr. McDonough is dead."

"Okay. We knew that might happen—"

But then Johnny began to sob.

"Hey," I said, "he had a stroke. You know how serious—"

"—He was dead when they brought him in! My dad brought a dead body to the hospital!"

"Well, Jesus, what were they supposed to do—shove him out in the snow when he died? Leave him by the side of the road?"

"Why didn't they turn back? If Mr. McDonough was already dead . . ."

The thought had occurred to me as well, yet I tried to defend the doctor. "After coming through that storm? I don't know about you, but I'm sure as hell in no hurry to hit the road again."

Johnny shook his head and continued to sob. I wanted to say something to comfort him, but couldn't think of what that might be. I couldn't believe he cared this deeply about Dale McDonough. I took out my cigarettes, shook one out in his direction, and held it there until he took it. When the car lighter popped out, I held its glowing orange rings toward him. You can't light a cigarette while you're crying like a baby. The incongruity alone will bring you up short. Johnny inhaled deeply and instantly calmed down.

"What else did they say in the hospital? Besides the fact that Mr. McDonough is dead."

"I still can't believe it. He was alive just this morning. Right there in the hotel."

"Okay, but believe it or not, it happened. Now what?"

Johnny's tears had stopped, but he continued to sniffle and wipe his nose on the back of his glove. "You know what this means?" he said. "He died in our car. I wonder if they knew, or if . . . Hell, I hope he didn't suffer too much."

I gave him another moment to allow his confused feelings to congeal, and then I reached over, grabbed his shoulder, and shook him. "That was your dad's car back there, you know. He's here. He and Louisa are here in Bellamy. Mr. McDonough is dead, but your dad's here."

He clapped his hand over mine. At first I thought he would push my hand away, but instead—for a second, maybe two—he just covered my hand with his, both of us holding onto Johnny Dunbar. Then he didn't remove my hand so much as lean away from my grasp.

"I know what's going on, Matt. I'm not that goddamn stupid. It's just that I don't . . . I don't want . . ." His voice caught, and he seemed close to tears again. Then suddenly he said, "I don't want Louisa to be my stepmother!"

We both knew that he hadn't expressed his misery very well—the issue of maternity wasn't what was troubling him, after all—but it was close enough. For Johnny to leap from denial to an outright statement of fear that his father was fucking Louisa Lindahl would have been too much.

"Well, hell, you don't want to be telling me about this— let's go find your dad and you can tell him how you feel!"

Before Johnny could articulate all that was wrong with that suggestion, I put the car in drive and sped away from the hospital, the Valiant's tires slipping on the packed snow and the car's back end swishing from side to side like a horse's tail.

I pulled into the Wagon Wheel's lot, and as I drove slowly down the line of cabins I noticed that the units were log constructions, but they'd been painted white to look less rustic. In every cabin the curtains were drawn, and no light glowed behind them. I parked next to the doctor's Imperial, leaving the Dunbar vehicles arranged exactly as they would have been in the family's garage.

"How do you want to do this?" I asked.

"I don't know."

"You want me to come in with you, or should I wait in the car again?"

Any enthusiasm he might have had for this undertaking had melted away. "How do I know he's here?"

"There's his goddamn car. It's the only one in the lot. If he's not in cabin eight, he's in number nine. Just go knock on the door. If he doesn't answer, knock on the other one."

But Johnny still didn't get out. He reached over and hit the horn ring. A scream couldn't have done a better job of violating the quiet winter air. He pressed it again before I could knock his hand away.

"What the hell are you doing?"

"I'm giving them a chance to stop whatever they're doing."

"That's real thoughtful of you. But that was loud enough to stop folks on the other side of town from what they're doing."

Johnny took a deep breath and opened the door.

"You want me to come with you?" I asked again.

He turned back to me with a look colder than anything the north wind had blown my way. "You might as well. That's what you're here for, isn't it? To see her?" He wasn't stupid. I climbed out of the car and trailed after my friend like a dog who had no will but its master's.

Before we could knock on the door of cabin eight, its curtains fluttered, a light went on inside, and the door opened. There was Dr. Dunbar. I'd just seen a look on his son's face that I'd never seen before, and now the father wore an equally unfamiliar expression. There was anger, certainly, but also befuddlement—as if, for the first time in his life, Rex Dunbar didn't know what he should say or do next.

"Johnny? *Johnny?* What the hell are you doing here?" The doctor was no longer wearing the suit and tie he'd worn that morning to church. He answered the door in stocking feet, trousers, and an undershirt. Immediately his glance traveled past both his son and me, as if he were trying to see through the car's frosted windows and determine whether his wife had also made this journey.

"Mom said we should find you. . . ."

"I talked to your mother not an hour ago. She didn't say

anything about you. . . ." He pulled his hand back through his hair, but his curls failed to settle back in place. "You drove through that storm?"

Johnny said, "It wasn't that bad," then stopped himself. "Mom was scared. She was worried that you might have gone off the road or something."

The doctor's wide shoulders blocked the doorway, but I tried to look inside the room. She was in there, I knew she was.

"Your mother knew this was an emergency. She knew I had to—. Oh, hell. I'll have to go through all this again with her anyway." Then he glanced back over his shoulder as if he noticed where I was staring. "Come on inside while I figure out what the hell we're going to do."

The cabin's only light came from a floor lamp with a yellowed lamp shade, so every corner remained in shadow. The logs that had been whitewashed on the cabin's exterior were left unpainted on the interior, and those heavy rolls of dark varnished wood—complete with knotholes and splinters—made it feel almost as if we'd stepped into a dim forest grove.

Most of the floor was covered with ratty, threadbare carpet, but an incongruous rectangle of linoleum protruded from under the bed. The bed was a double, covered with a blue and white striped pincord spread. The pillows barely made a bump at the head of the bed, and an army green wool blanket was folded at the foot. After careful but very quick study, I concluded that the bed's covering had not been pulled back, but it was also possible that the spread had been hastily smoothed.

There was no closet, but a tubular steel rack had been screwed to one of the logs, and there hung the doctor's suit coat, shirt, and tie. His overcoat was flung over a sagging, stained armchair, and under the coat's tweed two other fabrics peeked out—the red and black plaid of Louisa's mackinaw and the floral print of her dress.

I found this pile of clothing suggestive. First, off came Louisa's coat and then her dress. Only after she was down to her slip, bra, and panties, did the doctor remove his overcoat. After all, while Louisa's clothes could be carelessly tossed aside, the doctor's garments—purchased, of course, in Minneapolis or Chicago—had to be carefully hung. I couldn't see shoes or boots anywhere, but they could have been hurriedly kicked under the bed once it was discovered that the doctor's son was outside. The bathroom door was closed, and inside was Louisa Lindahl. Of that I had no doubt.

Across from the bed was a tall chest of drawers, and resting on top was a pint of Jim Beam. I couldn't see how much was in the bottle, but the warm smell of whiskey hung in the air. It was Sunday, and no bars or liquor stores were open; the doctor must have brought the bottle with him. I didn't see any glasses, so that meant he and Louisa drank right from the bottle. Or perhaps Louisa had a glass in the bathroom.

"We went to the hospital," Johnny told his father. "They told me that Mr. McDonough passed away."

The doctor walked over to the bedside table, which was not really a table at all, but rather a ladder-back chair with a spindle missing. On its surface were the doctor's pocket watch, his package of Chesterfields, his lighter, and an ashtray that already held a few cigarette butts. Dr. Dunbar shook out a cigarette and lit it.

"Dale died about halfway here. Wouldn't have made a

damn bit of difference if we'd gotten him here in minutes instead of hours. That was a massive cerebral hemorrhage. Massive."

"Does anyone else know? Mrs. McDonough?"

"Your mother knows. I told her to call Anna."

"So you didn't even have to bring him here. . . ."

"I didn't know that, son."

"But you knew how bad it was. . . ."

Dr. Dunbar sat on the edge of the bed, reached under, and brought out his shoes. "That's something you'll learn as a physician." While he stepped into his shoes, he held his cigarette between his lips, angling it upward to keep the smoke out of his eyes. "You try. Even when you know it's futile, you try."

"I can't be a doctor."

Johnny's statement jerked my head in his direction, but the doctor seemed unsurprised. He took his cigarette from his mouth. "You can't be. That's an interesting way of putting it," the doctor said. "When did you come to this decision?"

"I guess I've always known."

"But you chose this occasion to tell me." He shook his head, a gesture composed of equal parts amusement and disgust. Then he clapped his hands on his knees. "So. It's a day of revelations."

"Or confessions," replied Johnny. Considering how re- luctant he was to knock on the door in the first place, once inside he'd found an impressive supply of courage.

"Or confessions. Fine. You seem to have all the an- swers today." He stamped his feet hard and then he stood. "We can talk about this some other time."

"I've said all I have to say." The blotches on Johnny's cheeks darkened to a red that looked like clumsily smeared rouge.

"Ah, the man who knows his own mind and says what he says and then no more." Dr. Dunbar smiled derisively at his son. "Have it your way. You're mistaken if you think I have something riding on this." Then the doctor turned to me. "If you have any career plans, Matt, you can keep them to yourself. I'm at the point where I don't much give a good goddamn." He stubbed out his cigarette. "If I ever did."

He marched toward the door. "Let's go see if they have a room for you. And one for Louisa. They didn't have anything earlier. And we'll call your mother again and tell her you're here."

"I promised Matt a meal," said Johnny.

Dr. Dunbar looked at me as if he'd barely registered my presence before this moment. "Nothing's open," he said, and continued out the door.

The door had just closed behind Johnny and his father when Louisa stepped out of the bathroom. She must have expected the room to be empty, but she didn't startle when she saw me. She made no effort to cover herself—she was wearing nothing but a slip—or to explain why she was in the doctor's room. But her expression suggested that she assumed I knew everything.

"Hello, Matt. Are you here to rescue me?"

"Mrs. Dunbar was worried."

"Oh, I'm sure she was. I'm sure."

"But I guess you're safe and sound."

She smiled. The tendons in her neck showed, and her lower teeth gleamed. "Safe and sound."

*What will you do that Mrs. Dunbar won't?* That question had often pushed itself to the front of my mind even while I was supposed to be concentrating on keeping the car on the icy road, and it was more insistent now that I was in Louisa's presence. But since I couldn't ask that, I settled for another question.

"So, what's it like to haul a dead man through a blizzard?"

She walked around the bed and picked up Dr. Dunbar's pack of cigarettes. She shook one out and lit it, and nothing in her actions suggested that the cigarettes were not hers or her brand, or that my question had unnerved her in the least. "You know what was strange?" She exhaled toward the ceiling. "I was in the backseat with him when he was, you know, breathing his last breath, or however you want to say it—"

"—How does Dr. Dunbar say it?"

She paused for a moment. "Died, I think. Yeah, died. That's all."

Exactly right. I remembered a little talk Dr. Dunbar once had with Johnny and me, after he'd tried—and failed—to save Carl Oslund, a hunter who'd sliced through his femoral artery when he was field dressing a deer. The doctor had just returned to the house after speaking to Carl's parents. "Don't hide behind medical language," the doctor told us. "People have a hard enough time understanding when they're nervous or under pressure. Just give it to them straight. Bled to death. Died. Not exsanguinated. Not expired."

"Anyway," Louisa continued, "when Mr. McDonough was choking—which isn't exactly what happened because he didn't really have enough breath to choke—it made me think of Lester. When he died, I mean. When they first told me Lester killed himself in his cell, I thought, good. Good riddance to the sonofabitch. Serves him right. But then when I saw Mr. McDonough dying—and really not wanting to—I thought, poor Lester. Doing that all alone. . . . And if there was anything Lester wasn't good at, it was being alone. So I held Mr. McDonough close and watched him go. And then right at the end, when his eyes started kind of staring off, I realized that no matter what, when you're dying, you're alone." She shrugged. "There it is. To answer your question, it was a fucking picnic. But why ask me? You and Johnny came through it. You know. Just add a dying man and there you have it."

"Dr. Dunbar and Johnny went to see if they could find a room for you."

"And you," said Louisa. "Yeah, I heard. They won't have any trouble getting a room. No trouble at all."

"Johnny's pretty upset. He thinks his dad isn't going to be his dad anymore."

"He'll get over it." She sat down on the edge of the bed. Her shoes were under the bed too, and one was revealed when Louisa disturbed the bedspread. She bent over to push the shoe back, and when she did I could see down the front of her slip. Her breasts weighed down and strained against the slip's thin fabric. She started to sit back up, but when she realized where my gaze was focused, she stopped. Her body was slightly angled, so only one breast was fully exposed, allowing me to see once again that mauve nipple I'd first seen on Thanksgiving Day. In the cabin's dim light the aureole looked almost purple, more like a bruise than the small, stippled circle of flesh it was. Still, her power over me could only increase so long as she remained in that position.

"You can help Johnny," Louisa said. "You've made out fine without a father."

"It doesn't have to happen."

She arched her eyebrows. "Matthew. Don't you think it already has?"

"You could leave."

Louisa's laughter was icier than the wind that had blown all day. "Leave? Where the hell am I supposed to go? And why would I want to?"

Louisa leaned back on the bed, propping herself up on her elbows. When she did, her slip rode up above her knees. She had two slips—I'd seen the other one earlier in her dresser drawer—and this was the better one, worn to church on Sunday and then to a motel with a man whose marriage she hoped to destroy.

I had seen Louisa Lindahl's breasts, her scar, her torn underwear. I'd heard her secrets, and I knew her lies. But when I'd read her list for self-improvement, I felt as if her soul had been revealed to me. Once my eyes had traveled down that paper with its third-grade handwriting and its determined plan to advance her station in life through imitation and force of will, I felt as if I'd made Louisa Lindahl mine. No one could understand her the way I did.

"Come on," I said, reaching a hand out to her.

She took my hand, perhaps assuming that she was going along with a joke. "Where are we going?"

"Didn't you say you wanted to go to Denver?"

"Someday—"

"—So let's go."

She allowed herself to be pulled to her feet, but then she must have seen something in my eyes, something that told her how serious I was, and she tried to tug herself free of my grasp.

By then it was too late. I had a hold of her—it was my last chance, the doctor would be back any minute now, and I wasn't letting go—

"Come on," I said. "Let's go. I've still got the keys to the car. We'll be a hundred miles from here before they even figure out what to do."

I pulled and she pulled back. "Cut it out, Matthew. This isn't funny."

"I'm serious. You want to go to Denver. We can do it together."

This was as close as I could come to a declaration of love, but Louisa wasn't having it. "Goddamn it, Matthew! You're hurting me!"

I released her wrist, but before she could break away from me I grabbed her around the waist and pulled her tight to my side. Louisa was not a small woman, but she couldn't do anything to check our progress toward the cabin door.

She tried reasoning with me. "Matthew—stop. Please! We can't do this!"

Instead of resisting, she tried collapsing through my arms. She almost succeeded in this, but I pulled her back to her feet.

The door opened, and Johnny and the cold air came in together. I was so far gone that I almost asked my friend to help by grabbing Louisa's dress and coat. But I stopped myself, remembering that during his absence my friend had become my enemy.

"Jesus Christ, Matt—what the hell are you doing?"

There was no satisfactory way to answer his question. The doctor understood that and didn't bother saying a word. He rushed in right behind Johnny, and used his forward momentum to put even more force into a punch that would have been plenty powerful if he'd swung flat-footed. His fist caught me just above the temple, and I was on my way down before I fully comprehended that I'd been hit. I crumbled to the floor as Dr. Dunbar shouted, "You sonofabitch! You stupid meddling sonofabitch!"

I tried to gather myself and get to my feet, but then another blow to the head knocked me back down. Had the doctor kicked me? Had Johnny? I heard the doctor say, "Out! I want him the hell out of here!"

My lips and nose went numb, and darkness crowded the edges of my vision. I was losing consciousness and I knew it. The doctor used to counsel putting your head between your knees if you believed you were going to pass out, but what was I supposed to do when I was already on the floor?

I rolled away from the most recent blow, but before I could do anything more to move out of danger, someone grabbed my feet and began dragging me toward the open door. I tried to kick free, but four hands were now gripping my ankles. Somehow I'd brought father and son together, uniting them in a single effort. Johnny had ahold of one leg and his father had the other.

My coat was open, my sweater and shirt rode up, and my stomach's bare flesh burned as they towed me across the threadbare carpet. It was the doctor's plain intention to throw me out in the snow, and there was nothing I could do about it.

My chin banged on the doorsill as they dragged me across it. I tried again to grab ahold of something, but I succeeded only in snapping a fingernail and abrading both palms on the frame's rough wood.

They kept pulling until I was closer to the cars than the cabin, and then they let go—simultaneously, as if a signal had passed between father and son. Any thought I had of getting up was abruptly quelled when Dr. Dunbar pinned me in the snow by putting his foot on the back of my neck.

In the next I felt the pressure of a foot on my back, too. Because the pressure wasn't substantial enough to be the doctor's, the other foot had to be Johnny's. The son imitating the father, he pressed my pelvis down as if to grind into the snow the part of me that had been responsible for sundering our friendship.

Father and son kept me down long enough for me to be reminded again as to who possessed power and weight in the world. And then they stepped off me—again, simultaneously.

Dr. Dunbar left me with parting words: "Now you stay out here. Stay out until that fucking hot blood of yours cools off, and you're fit for human company!"

## 19.

I DIDN'T BOTHER TRYING TO GET UP until I heard the door close, and I could be sure they were back inside the cabin. My clothes were wet, my face was throbbing, and I started to shiver.

But I had no intention of staying there. Nor would I howl or claw at the door. I fumbled around with my stiff, freezing fingers until I found the keys to the Valiant in my pocket. I climbed into the car, started it up, and put it into reverse. I backed into a snowdrift, but then I put the car in drive and slammed the accelerator to the floor. The tires churned and spun in the snow, but finally found their traction and I sped away from the Wagon Wheel. If I'd known the way to Denver—or to Minneapolis or Winnipeg—I might have driven in that direction. As it was, I headed back toward Willow Falls.

Sure that I would soon see the pursuing headlights of the doctor's Chrysler in the rearview mirror, or even the flashing red lights of a county sheriff or highway patrolman, I drove as fast as I dared. Curves came up before I could slow for them, and I often veered over into the oncoming lane. I hit icy stretches of road before I could prepare for them. But as long as the highway be-hind me was dark, I was free, and my speed only made that state more exhilarating, though that state had to be temporary. In addition to any other offenses, I was now a car thief.

Obviously, I no longer had any hope of a life with Louisa Lindahl. But even as I admitted that to myself, I had to smile at the thought. As if I'd ever had a chance! I never would come closer to Louisa Lindahl than I had when she'd lain anesthetized on the doctor's table. The other occasions of contact had been stolen, forced, or inconsequential. The kiss had been nothing but mockery. I'd believed that I could compete with a grown man, and a man of power and stature at that, a man of intelligence and charm and good looks. I wasn't going to Denver with or without Louisa. I was heading back to my home-town, and once there, I'd park the Valiant right where it belonged—in the Dunbars' driveway. Then I'd walk home in the cold once again, and climb into my own bed and wait for the punishment that was sure to come my way. The best I could wish for was that I'd fall asleep quickly, so I wouldn't have to lie awake and think about what a self-deluding fool I'd been.

Fast in the track of these realizations came a strange sensation. A calm suffused me, and it was composed of equal parts resignation and hope. As I covered the lonely miles, hunched over the steering wheel, the feeling that came over me was similar to what I'd felt driving in the other direction, when the wind subsided and the snow faded—*maybe I'll make it.*

The car's heater provided enough warmth to stop the

rattling from the chills I'd had since being stomped into the snow. I leaned back and eased up on the gas.

That was when it happened.

The sudden deceleration might have caused the tires to lose their bite. Maybe I touched the brakes. Perhaps I hit a patch of black ice. Whatever the cause, the Valiant suddenly went out of control, revolving furiously down the highway. If another car had been coming, I'd have been helpless to prevent a collision.

Eventually the car stopped spinning, only to slide backward into a snow-filled ditch. For a moment I sat there, unable to believe my luck, and paralyzed by thoughts that canceled each other out. *You could have been killed. Now you'll never get away.*

I knew what I'd find when I climbed out of the car. A few trees stood near the road, and their remnant bur oak leaves chattered in the wind. A coil of snow tumbled across the highway. Overhead a near-full moon glowed with a pale, cold light. The stars glittered like chips of mica in a black road. Somewhere, at a distance beyond sight, a wood fire kept someone warm, and that aroma found its way to me. Exactly as I'd feared, the car was sunk in snow up to its doors. In the trunk was the shovel I'd made Johnny pack, but I had no idea where to begin, or whether it would do any good.

I gave up. Either the doctor would come along or I'd freeze, and I was so cold and tired that the first option didn't seem so awful.

At just that moment, a car approached. I had an impulse to leap into the ditch, high-step through the snow, and hide among the trees. But I stood my ground, and the car's headlights cast my shadow back toward Bellamy. It was an old Hudson, with piles of snow clinging improbably to its sloping lines. It stopped next to me and the Valiant, though the driver made no attempt to pull over to the side of the road. The passenger's frost-covered window rolled down, but it was the driver who shouted out to me.

"You got trouble, ain't you?"

"I sure do."

"You ain't hurt?"

"No."

"Where you going?"

"Willow Falls."

"You're pointed the wrong way."

The man in the passenger seat removed his hat, as if its brim might be blocking the conversation.

"I know," I said.

"How long you been stuck?"

"Just a few minutes."

"So you ain't froze."

"Not yet."

The Hudson's engine misfired, coughed, and threatened to die, but the driver gunned it and kept it running.

"You got money?" he asked. "We could get you out of that ditch for the right price."

"Only a couple bucks."

He laughed. "Then I guess that's the right price!" The Hudson's gears clashed, and he eased the car onto the shoulder.

In spite of the cold, the two men who climbed out of the car were in shirtsleeves. In the moonlight I could see that the passenger, a slender, stooped man, was walking slowly and grimacing as if he were in pain. But the driver was big and robust enough for both of them. He looked like a grizzly bear shaved and made to wear a T-shirt. Both men were Indians.

Like almost everyone who grew up in our corner of Minnesota in that day and age, I had been exposed to plenty of anti-Indian bigotry during my formative years. As part of this instruction in racism, we were taught to be wary and perhaps even fearful in our dealings with Indians. But even if I had taken those lessons to heart—and I hadn't—I wouldn't have cared that night. What could they do—rob me of the few dollars I was going to give them anyway? Steal the car that wasn't mine? Beat me up? The side of my face was swollen from the doctor's fist, and the small of my back ached from the pressure of his foot. I had nothing to fear from these two.

Together we walked back to inspect the Valiant. The Indians smelled of wood smoke, whiskey, and cigarettes.

"Yep," said the bear-man. "High-centered. You're in there good." But this was not the expression of hopelessness it might have seemed. "You and me'll push," he said, "and Barney'll drive. He's sick, so he's got to take it easy."

Barney was bending over even farther.

"What's the matter?"

"Bellyache. He'll be off his feed for a couple days and then he'll be fine."

Barney obviously objected to having his condition minimized in this way. "Bellyache!" he growled. "Feels like I been gut shot!"

"You ever been?" Barney's friend asked.

Barney said nothing.

"Then I guess you can't say, can you?"

Then we stopped and listened. A car was approaching, the whine of its engine sounding at first like a taut wire vibrating in the wind. When I realized it was coming from Willow Falls and not Bellamy, I relaxed. Headlights swept around the curve of the highway ahead of the car, and then it appeared. The driver saw us and slowed. And then something—the depth to which the Valiant was sunk, the presence of two Indians along the road, the lateness of the hour, the quickening cold—changed the driver's mind, and he sped up again.

Barney grunted and crossed his arms over his abdomen.

The big Indian asked me, "Got a flashlight?"

"I don't know."

"You don't know!" He found my answer hilarious, and his laugh boomed out across the dark snowy plains.

"It's . . . my mother's car."

That was even funnier to him. "Barney, look in his mother's glove box and see if his mother's got a flashlight like a mother's supposed to have."

By this time Barney had folded himself into the car. "Nope," he called out. "No flashlight."

The big Indian stepped into the ditch behind the car, and I followed. My shoes and socks were already soaked. "What the hell," he said. "It don't much matter. If we gotta push, we gotta push."

"There's a shovel in the trunk."

"Yeah? We'll try muscle power first."

The snow was not as deep behind the car as it was in front. We positioned ourselves at each side of the back bumper, ready to push once Barney started the engine and put the car in gear.

"Okay," the big Indian said to me, "get ready to step back. Barney's going to rock it—drive, reverse, drive, reverse. Kind of like dancing."

Barney couldn't have heard this and no signal passed between the men, but right at that moment, as if on cue, the Valiant stuttered once, then roared to life. I was standing over the exhaust pipe, and fumes rose to my face. I placed my hands on the car's trunk and felt its cold metal right through my gloves. I was ready to put my back into it—a chance for physical release after the frustration and humiliation of the beating at the hands of Dr. Dunbar and his son.

We pushed and pushed, but the Valiant didn't move more than an inch or two forward. Then backward, when Barney shifted into reverse to try to find a spot where there might be a little traction. The rear wheels whined and spun in place, spitting snow up into our faces. The smell of burning rubber and automobile exhaust overpowered the odor of the big Indian's whiskey breath.

Two more cars passed while we were heaving and straining against the Valiant's trunk, but neither stopped. The second car slowed, and I eased up in my grunting effort to glance in its direction. A boy looked out at us from the backseat, his face as pale as moonlit snow. I thought I saw his lips move, and I imagined him telling the driver they should stop. But the car sped by, and my glimpse of him lasted no longer than my glimpse of Louisa Lindahl's bare breasts.

As if that passing car told him once and for all that the car would never leave the ditch with the help of any hands except those that were already on it, the big Indian said, "The hell with it. Let's get this fucker out of here."

Barney punched the transmission into gear once again, and his big friend heaved hard, releasing a sound that was equal parts grunt, roar, and scream. *"Heerr-ahh!"* And before its echo died away, he damn near lifted the Valiant out of its ruts. Instead of helping push the car free, I was soon being pulled along behind it. The wheels spun and whined and churned up more snow, but Barney managed to drive the car out of the ditch.

And he kept on going, cruising down the highway for a good fifty yards or so before the brake lights blinked on and the car glided to a stop at the side of the road.

My momentum was already carrying me that way, so I ran after the car while the man who had been strong enough to heave the car clear stood in the snow and gasped for air.

When I caught up to the Valiant, Barney's head was thrown back and his hat had fallen into the backseat. His eyes were closed, and he was trying to bring his knees up toward his chest.

I opened the car door and the dome light came on. Barney didn't even glance at me. He was too busy biting back his pain and shaking with chills.

Instinctively, I put my hand to his forehead. "Damn— you're burning up!"

Barney smiled through his pain. "And he says it's just a bellyache."

"A fever means infection. . . . Where did you say the pain was?"

"Down here," he said, indicating the position of his hands on his abdomen.

"Lower right quadrant. . . . Have you been vomiting?"

"I puked a couple hours ago. But I haven't ate much, so there ain't much to bring up."

"Diarrhea?"

Barney closed his eyes again and shook his head. "Huh-uh."

The big Indian caught up to us, and he stood behind me, looking over my shoulder at his ailing friend. "Gettin' worse, Barney?"

Barney nodded and slid lower in his seat.

"You could have appendicitis," I suggested.

"Nah," Barney said. "The army already took my appendix out. For free."

"Okay, okay. Let me think. Pain in the lower right abdomen. Guarding. Fever. Chills."

"Fuckin-A he's got chills," the big Indian said. "What's the goddamn temperature? Ten?" He stamped up and down and flapped his arms. "I got chills. Hell, we all got chills."

"This is different," I said. "Barney, will you do something? Will you lie down across the front seat?"

"He lays down," the other man said, "he ain't going to want to get up."

But Barney complied. He stretched out across the seat, a shudder coursing through him as if he'd just tossed back a shot of whiskey.

"Okay, Barney—" When Dr. Dunbar treated a patient gripped hard by illness or injury, he made a point of saying the patient's name as often as possible. It was a way, the doctor used to say, "of keeping the patient in the world."

"Here's what I want you to do," I said to Barney. "I know your stomach hurts, but I want you to put your hand, okay, both your hands, right over the spot that hurts the worst."

Barney did as I asked.

"All right, Barney. Now press down right there. Right on the spot. Okay, good. Keep pressing. A little harder. Now, when I tell you, take your hands away. Fast. Okay—now!"

Barney was an obedient patient, even when everything I asked him to do caused him pain. And the last step was agonizing.

He jerked his hands away on command and instantly cried out. "Oooh! Goddamn!"

His knees jerked upward and he twisted so hard to the side he almost toppled off the car seat.

Just as I'd expected. Blumberg's sign. Dr. Dunbar had told us about it as a test for peritonitis when a perforated bowel almost killed Harley Platt, the owner of a butcher shop in Willow Falls. Then Dr. Dunbar made Johnny and me lie down, each in turn, while he pressed on our abdomens and showed us how to check for rebound tenderness.

I reached into the car and grabbed Barney's ankle, bare above his oxford, its cracked worn leather his only protection against snow and cold. I wasn't trying to control him; I was trying to comfort him, though I had no idea whether I had that power.

In a voice as gentle as I owned, I said, "How are you doing, Barney? Okay?"

Through his pain, Barney managed a smile. He was too polite to say anything about the stupidity of my question. "Okay," he said, and struggled to sit up again.

I motioned for Barney's friend to join me behind the car. There, both of us eerily illuminated by the car's taillights, I said, "Your friend's in bad shape. He's got an infection that's making him really sick. He has to go to a hospital."

He nodded, his smile dimming for the first time. "I'll see how he's doing tomorrow. If he ain't better I'll take him to the VA hospital."

"No," I said firmly. "Tomorrow's no good. It will be too late. Your friend's got peritonitis. He's only going to get worse. This is an emergency. You have to go to the hospital in Bellamy. And you have to drive like hell to get there."

Barney was out of the car now and limping toward us. I don't know if he'd heard the word "peritonitis," but he knew we were talking about his condition.

"Hey," Barney said, "are you a doctor or something?"

The wind seemed to die as the snowy plains around us waited for my answer.

"No," I said. "But my father was."

## 20.

I DIDN'T RUSH BACK TO WILLOW FALLS, and not just because I was shaken after spinning out and sliding off the road. I couldn't handle any more suspense. If Dr. Dunbar was speeding after me and his wife's car, I was ready to be overtaken. If law enforcement was on my trail, I was ready to be caught.

But I saw just two other cars on the drive back to Willow Falls, and neither driver displayed any interest in me. The streets of my hometown were snow packed and drifted over, but completely quiet, and I drove the Valiant back to where it belonged.

Lights burned in a few windows of the Dunbar home. Was Mrs. Dunbar waiting up? Didn't she know that neither her husband, nor her son, nor Louisa Lindahl was likely to return to their own bed that night? Didn't she realize that when they did return none would be the person who left? And for that matter, did she have any sense that though she was comfortable and warm in a place with light and heat, her house had been blown apart as surely as if the afternoon's winds had flattened every wall that sheltered her?

The driveway was partially cleared—perhaps the result of the twins' enthusiastic but inefficient shoveling—but I managed to park the Valiant in its usual spot in the garage. When Johnny and I left the house that afternoon, the wind had stacked snow on the porch so high we practically had to climb over a drift to leave. But during our absence the wind had shifted and now the path in and out of the back door was as clear as July. I entered quietly and paused in the kitchen to announce my presence. "Hello," I said. "It's Matt. Anyone up?"

No one answered. I slipped off my shoes and padded into the house's quiet, warm interior. In each room I called out softly, but there was no response.

I found Mrs. Dunbar in the living room, asleep on the couch. On the table next to her was an ashtray brimming with lipstick-stained cigarette butts smoked right down to the filter, and the cup she had been drinking coffee from didn't have a saucer.

I probably could have crept through the house and completed my mission without waking Mrs. Dunbar or her daughters, but I didn't want to take a chance. For a moment I stared at her. Her hair was mussed, her mouth was open, and her skirt had ridden up above her knees. *What won't you do that Louisa will?*

"Mrs. Dunbar," I whispered.

She was stretched out on the couch and didn't stir. She was wearing the clothes she had worn that morning to church, and her pearl necklace—those omnipresent pearls—were twisted and tugged tight to her throat.

I crouched down beside her, close enough to hear her breathing. "Mrs. Dunbar?" I said, louder this time.

She came awake suddenly, but without a physical start, as if her body lagged well behind her mind. Her eyes blinked open, and she recognized me. "Matt?" she said, but she was already looking past me.

"I came alone," I said. "I was afraid my mom would be worried, so I drove back in your car. The others will come later tonight or tomorrow morning."

"Johnny—?"

"Johnny's with them." It took a moment for the import of what I told her to take hold, but once it did, her relief was visible.

"He decided to ride back with his dad," I added.

"I called your mother earlier—"

"Yeah, but I just thought it would be better if I came back sooner rather than later. You know. She worries. Because of what happened with my dad."

She smiled kindly at me and sat up, careful to tug her skirt down in the process. "You're a good son, Matt."

I stood up. "Well, I don't know about that . . ."

"And a good friend to Johnny. When the two of you left this afternoon I wasn't worried because the two of you were going. I knew Johnny would be all right with you along."

There was so much I could have said. *You didn't send both of us; you sent Johnny and you didn't know, at least not at first, that I'd go along. And did you really believe that Johnny would be all right?* But what was the point? I knew very well what Mrs. Dunbar was doing. She was smoothing her skirt and rearranging the collar of her blouse and straightening up the past, bringing it all in line with who she had to be. Like Louisa, like me, Mrs. Dunbar had her own list of what she had to do in order to create herself in her own image. Though she didn't have to write anything down.

"Johnny drove," I said. "I was just along for the ride."

The room was dark, but Mrs. Dunbar saw something darker. "Matt, is that a bruise? On the side of your face?"

She reached up tentatively, and I wanted to crouch down again, to come close, to feel her cool fingers where my head still throbbed from her husband's fist, to feel a mother's touch. . . .

"I slipped getting out of the car in Bellamy. Fell right on my face."

"If Rex were here he could take a look at it."

"He already did. He said I should be more careful."

"I have an aspirin. . . ."

"No, it's okay. It doesn't hurt. It was mostly just embarrassing."

Mrs. Dunbar smiled up at me. She now had her ankles crossed. "It was very cute earlier. The twins wanted to stay up late, until you and Johnny came back. That's what they said: Until Johnny and Matt come back, please? Not their father. Not just Johnny. Johnny and Matt."

At any other time I might have been touched by her remark. There were times when I came close to forgetting that Janet and Julia were not my little sisters, too. But it was late, I was tired, and I still had something I needed to do before my night came to a close. "Yeah. Cute. But hey, I need to go upstairs and pick up something and then I'll be on my way, okay?"

"Would you like me to give you a ride?"

The Dunbars . . . always ready to give me a ride. "That's

all right," I said. "You have to stay with the twins. Besides, it's not far."

As I climbed the stairs, I kept to the side of each step so they were less likely to creak. I stayed close to the wall as I tread carefully down the halls, and I turned the doorknob slowly, trying to make as little noise as possible. Mrs. Dunbar knew I was there. The twins were not likely to wake. It was the house itself I was trying not to disturb. I took what I came for and made my way out as quietly as I could.

## 21.

MY LIFE KEPT MAKING ragged duplicates of itself.

Before I went to bed that night I examined my swollen face in the bathroom mirror, another injury that had come at the hands of Rex Dunbar. But I didn't look or puzzle long over the bruise or the how and why of it. This time I was sure of the motive behind the blow.

And once again I was waiting, just as I had done after New Year's Eve, when Dr. Dunbar predicted consequences that never came. This time, however, I felt better equipped for what might come. When the doctor burst into the motel room and punched me I'd been completely unprepared for the blow, but I swore I wouldn't be blindsided again.

But Monday came and Dr. Dunbar didn't knock on our door, ready to kick my ass again. He didn't pull up to the curb as I was walking to school, or leap from his big Chrysler and pummel me. Nor did the sheriff show up to pull me out of class. Not that day or the next.

I couldn't relax though, because now I was waiting for Thursday. That was the day when Jay's Pancake House slid a few tables together at the back of the restaurant for the afternoon Kiwanis Club meeting, and the women's circle met in the basement of the First Presbyterian church. Dr. Dunbar belonged to the first organization, and Mrs. Dunbar the second.

On Thursday afternoon, shortly after lunch, when I felt confident both meetings were underway, I asked to be excused from my fifth-period history class. I told Mrs. Spires that I was sick to my stomach, and I said it with a grimace in the hopes of implying a messy urgency behind my request.

I had the car that day, so when I left the high school I was able to travel quickly to my destination. A light snow sifted down, as fine as cornmeal, which meant that I would leave a trail. But while that realization was upsetting, I also knew I couldn't cover every contingency, and I wasn't about to abandon my plan. Perhaps my footprints would mingle with the milkman's and the postman's, and perhaps as the snow continued to fall it would conceal my tracks rather than reveal them.

How many times had I entered the Dunbar house over the years? Thousands, certainly. Yet very seldom had I walked in through the front door, as I did that Thursday afternoon. I didn't bother to take off my coat, but I did pull off my overshoes. I was willing to leave my footprints in the snow leading up to the door, but I wouldn't dirty Mrs. Dunbar's floors.

I didn't have to search long before I found Louisa. She was sitting at the kitchen table, eating a ham sandwich and paging through a copy of *Look* magazine. A Chesterfield from the pack on the table burned in the ashtray, and there was a bottle of 7-Up open next to her.

She spotted me before I said a word, and once again, she didn't startle at my appearance. Maybe she had been expecting me to turn up. And maybe she had experienced so much in her life that she could no longer scare.

I was about to find out.

"Well, well. Look what the cat dragged in." Louisa put down her sandwich and picked up her cigarette. "Somehow I didn't think I'd heard the last of Matthew Garth. Come on in. Take a load off."

I didn't move. Not yet.

She smiled at me. "I don't suppose you brought me a Valentine, did you?" It suddenly dawned on me what day it was.

I stepped forward, but I didn't sit down.

"Ooh," Louisa winced. She was referring to the yellow and purple bruise coloring the side of my face. "He really nailed you, didn't he?"

I felt myself losing heart in her presence, so I rushed to my purpose for being there. "You're going to Denver," I said.

She smiled and raised her eyebrows. "Maybe. Someday. But right now"—she wriggled a bit as if the hard kitchen chair were as soft as an armchair and she could sink more deeply into it—"I like it here."

"Today," I said. "Denver. Or Minneapolis. Or Fargo. Or Sioux Falls. But somewhere."

I reached into my back pocket and took out my billfold. I counted out two fifties, six twenties, five tens, and seven fives, and laid them all out on the table. "That's enough to cover bus or train fare and arrive with some money in your pocket. The Greyhound leaves this afternoon at four o'clock. If you'd rather take the train, you can get on at Bellamy."

When I put my wallet back in my pocket I noticed how much thinner it was without those twenty bills.

"Goddamn. You are persistent, Matt. I'll say that for you. But me running off with you was about the stupidest, pie-in-the-fucking-sky notion before. And now my . . . prospects have improved. So that idea that didn't interest me in the least then has far less appeal now."

"We're not going to Denver," I said. "You. Alone. Today."

Louisa reached out and tapped through the pile of bills with her index finger. It was a casual, dismissive gesture. But it was also enough for her to see how much was there. "And this is supposed to persuade me? What is this—the money you were saving to buy a car? To pay for college? Did you save this up from your paper route?"

In fact, I'd taken the money that morning from an envelope in the top drawer of my dresser. The amount had fluctuated over the years, saved from doing odd jobs in the neighborhood—shoveling snow or mowing lawns or putting up storm windows—or from opening an annual birthday or Christmas card from my uncle and finding a five-dollar bill inside, or busing tables at Phil's. The money had always been important to me, and while I'd never hoarded it—I had no trouble taking money out to buy beer or take Debbie to a movie—I tried to replace what I took and add to the pile when I could. I never put any money in the bank, but when smaller bills accumulated, I took them to a teller at First National and converted them to larger denominations.

Still, when Louisa made that remark, it occurred to me that I'd never been saving the money for anything in particular. But people always needed money, whether it was to get through a day or a year, to last through a life or to start a new one.

"You better get packed," I said. "If you like, I can drive you to the station. Or even to the depot in Bellamy. But you have to get going now."

"Matt. Matt. You're stuck on the one note. Come on. Look around. Why would I want to leave this? This is as good as I've ever had it, and it's only going to get better."

I didn't have to look around. I knew that room and that house as well as any on the planet. I knew them better than Louisa Lindahl did.

"You're leaving"—I drew a breath and started over—"You're leaving because if you don't I'll tell Mrs. Dunbar—and mister too—that you've been scheming to . . . to take up with the doctor. To steal him away."

She smiled, and a look of relief crossed her face. She obviously thought she knew what I had, and to her it didn't look like much.

"You don't understand, Matt. That's not the way it works between men and women. I didn't steal him. He fell for me."

"I'll say it different."

"You can say it anyway you like. But, Matt"—if I didn't know better, I would have thought her puckered forehead indicated genuine concern—"why the hell would anyone believe you?"

I reached inside my coat pocket and touched the item that I'd gone upstairs to take the night I drove the Valiant back from Bellamy. Since then it had either been on my person or, while I slept, under my pillow.

Quickly, before I lost what little courage I had left, I pulled out the stenographic pad, held it aloft, and said, "Because of this."

Louisa didn't bother pretending. She knew what I held, what it was, and what it meant.

"That doesn't belong to you, Matt."

I was so uncertain and unsteady in this enterprise that I hid behind what I'd already said. "This is why you're leaving. Because if you don't, I'll tell the doctor and his wife what you've been scheming. This is proof, and we both know it."

Her smile returned, but its fragility was plain. "Show him. He won't care. . . ."

"If you believe that, then you don't know the man."

"That's not yours, Matt. It's not yours—" She lurched a little, as if she considered leaping up and trying to take the pad from me.

"It *was* yours, but I took it. Now it's mine. Sound familiar?"

"You really are a prick. You know that? A real prick." Color rose to her cheeks.

"Yes, ma'am, I've heard that. Now you need to go upstairs and pack your things."

Louisa took a moment to survey the room. She lingered over the big gas range, the refrigerator with its double doors. The breakfast dishes that had been washed and rinsed, then left to dry in the rack beside the sink. The money on the table. The half-eaten sandwich. The cigarettes. There was nothing there that could help her, unless it was a butcher knife in a drawer. I almost felt sorry for her.

But when she looked back at me it was with a smile and a plan better than the sharpest blade in the house.

"Why don't you come upstairs with me, Matt? We've got the house to ourselves." She glanced at the clock over the stove. "And time."

I shook my head. "Can't do it."

"You won't have to do anything. Just hang on tight. I'll do all the work."

"You *don't* have time. You have to pack."

"Do you get it? Do you fucking get it? Do you know what I'm offering you?"

"I believe you're proposing a business arrangement. Some sort of exchange—"

"—Don't be a fucking smart-ass, Matt."

It was my turn to look at the clock. "You have to get going."

"Matt . . ." The head-lowered, heavy-lidded look she gave me was supposed to be seductive, and I had no doubt she could usually convey that message very well. But something had slipped away from her, and the expression she wore now had too much desperation to be enticing. "We had some good times together," she continued. "I knew what you wanted. I always knew. And now you can have it. It can be like before, only with you and me—"

I just shook my head.

Louisa apparently sensed a greater intransigence in me than I felt. "Oh, fuck it," she said, and swept up the 305 dollars in one quick motion. "I'll be goddamned if I'll beg."

She was on her way out of the room when she wheeled about to face me once again. "You don't need to wait around. I'll find my own ride." Two steps up the maid's staircase she turned a final time. "And Matt? You can stick that steno pad up your ass for all I care."

Until that moment I had never seen Louisa Lindahl's

eyes glisten with tears. That she was capable of tears didn't mean she could be trusted, however. When I left the house, I got in the car and drove away, but then I circled around and parked on a hillside. From there I had a view—through the light, fine-grained snow, through a winter-bare stand of trees—of the front of the Dunbar house.

Within half an hour a car pulled up in front of the house. I recognized the driver as Hank Hettig, a fellow who might well have shared a booth with Louisa and Lester at PeeWee's Bar. He didn't get out of the car, but he didn't have to. Almost immediately Louisa came out the front door, chipboard suitcase in hand. She climbed into the car, and they drove off together.

I never saw Louisa Lindahl again, and as far as I know, she never returned to Willow Falls. Nor did I ever enter the Dunbar house again, not even when I came back to town after completing my education. By then that old Victorian mansion had been chopped up into apartments and offices, so its rooms would have served me well for both a residence and a clinic where I could practice medicine myself. I ended up leasing a home and an office in another part of town instead, not so much because I feared ghosts, but rather because the Dunbar house was already in need of repair.

But that afternoon when I kept watch on the Dunbar home from my hillside post, I felt as if I had saved both house and family from ruin. I was seventeen years old, the only child of a single working mother. I should have known better. There are destructive forces at loose in the world, from which neither buildings nor families can be saved.

The doctor was the first Dunbar to return that afternoon. Maybe he had a patient he had to see. And maybe he wanted to be with Louisa while they had the house to themselves. Once that big black Chrysler Imperial drove up, however, I drove away.

Dr. Dunbar left Willow Falls within a year, headed, so the story went, to Iowa to participate in a program in rural medicine sponsored by the University of Iowa. He was only supposed to be gone for a couple months, but when time passed and he didn't return, it was said that a small town in South Dakota had extended a very attractive offer, luring Dr. Dunbar to their community, where he would head up a brand-new clinic. Maybe this story was true. But when Mrs. Dunbar left Willow Falls with the children soon after, they went in the opposite direction, to Saint Paul, where her family lived. The house was soon for sale.

Maybe the good doctor and Louisa Lindahl remained in contact and reunited in that small South Dakota town. Or maybe he discovered elsewhere a woman—or women— who would do what Mrs. Dunbar wouldn't.

*I LAST SPOKE TO JOHNNY DUNBAR on that occasion when so many people exchange final words, although they seldom know or admit it at the time.*

*The night of our high school commencement was blustery and unseasonably cold. As we marched out of the auditorium, the wind found us even under our black gowns. A gust ripped loose a few flakes of snow, and in that instant our graduation was not the reason the date was notable. Instead, it became the day when something rarer occurred—snow in May, and in late May at that. It was the eighth consecutive month that snow fell on Willow Falls that year.*

*Our after-graduation party was held in an open field north of Frenchman's Forest. We would have built a bonfire no matter what, but we wouldn't have huddled around it for warmth the way we had to that night. And we surely would have been drinking anyway, but we might have stayed out until dawn had it not been so cold. As it was, the heart went out of our celebration early, and kids drifted off, pairing off with boyfriends or girlfriends, or heading home to warm beds.*

*Johnny Dunbar and I were among the last of the class of 1963 to remain by the fire, and when it was little more than embers and choking smoke, Johnny spoke the first words he had spoken to me since that night I fled from him and his father.*

*He was holding a bottle of beer, and he kicked something toward the fire. Then Johnny Dunbar said, "We could have been happy."*

*He said this with a look so fierce that I didn't argue with him. I didn't remind him that it was his father, his father and Louisa Lindahl, who had upset the balance of our lives. I didn't mention how long it had taken the bruises on my back to fade, bruises made by his boots when he ground me into the snow. And I didn't ask him who "we" were.*

## ACKNOWLEGMENTS

BIG THANKS TO EVERYONE AT MILKWEED: Ben Barnhart, Jennifer Harmening, Ethan Rutherford, Kate Strickland, Patrick Thomas, Allison Wigen, and of course Emilie Buchwald, who started it all.

A special thanks to Daniel Slager, my editor, for his intelligence, understanding, and keen eye.

Thanks to PJ Mark, my agent, for his friendship and support.

I will be forever indebted to Ralph Vicinanza and will miss his wisdom and laughter.

Thanks to Elly Heuring and Amy Watson.

Above all, thanks to Susan, to whom this novel is dedicated.

A slightly altered version of the first three chapters appeared in *The North American Review*.

LARRY WATSON is the author of *Montana 1948, Justice, White Crosses, Orchard,* and several other novels. He is the recipient of the Milkweed National Fiction Prize, the Friends of American Writers award, two fellowships from the National Endowment for the Arts, and many other prizes and awards. He teaches writing and literature at Marquette University in Milwaukee, where he lives with his wife, Susan.

For more, see larry-watson.com.

MORE FICTION FROM MILKWEED EDITIONS

To order books or for more information, contact
Milkweed at (800) 520-6455
or visit our Web site (www.milkweed.org).

*Driftless*
By David Rhodes

*The Farther Shore*
By Matthew Eck

*The Long-Shining Waters*
By Danielle Sosin

*Ordinary Wolves*
By Seth Kantner

*Vestments*
By John Reimringer

MILKWEED EDITIONS

Founded as a nonprofit organization in 1980, Milkweed Editions is an independent publisher. Our mission is to identify, nurture and publish transformative literature, and build an engaged community around it.

JOIN US

In addition to revenue generated by the sales of books we publish, Milkweed Editions depends on the generosity of institutions and individuals like you. In an increasingly consolidated and bottom-line-driven publishing world, your support allows us to select and publish books on the basis of their literary quality and transformative potential. Please visit our Web site (www.milkweed.org) or contact us at (800) 520-6455 to learn more.

Milkweed Editions, a nonprofit publisher, gratefully acknowledges sustaining support from Amazon.com; Emilie and Henry Buchwald; the Bush Foundation; the Patrick and Aimee Butler Foundation; Timothy and Tara Clark; the Dougherty Family Foundation; Friesens; the General Mills Foundation; John and Joanne Gordon; Ellen Grace; William and Jeanne Grandy; the Jerome Foundation; the Lerner Foundation; Sanders and Tasha Marvin; the McKnight Foundation; Mid-Continent Engineering; the Minnesota State Arts Board, through an appropriation by the Minnesota State Legislature and a grant from the National Endowment for the Arts; Kelly Morrison and John Willoughby; the National Endowment for the Arts; the Navarre Corporation; Ann and Doug Ness; Jörg and Angie Pierach; the Carl and Eloise Pohlad Family Foundation; the RBC Foundation USA; the Target Foundation; the Travelers Foundation; Moira and John Turner; and Edward and Jenny Wahl.

Interior design by Connie Kuhnz
Typeset in Warnock Pro
by BookMobile Design and Publishing Services
Printed on acid-free 100% postconsumer waste paper
by Friesens Corporation

## ENVIRONMENTAL BENEFITS STATEMENT

**Milkweed Editions** saved the following resources by printing the pages of this book on chlorine free paper made with 100% post-consumer waste.

| TREES | WATER | ENERGY | SOLID WASTE | GREENHOUSE GASES |
|:---:|:---:|:---:|:---:|:---:|
| 84 | 38,361 | 35 | 2,432 | 8,507 |
| FULLY GROWN | GALLONS | MILLION BTUs | POUNDS | POUNDS |

Environmental impact estimates were made using the Environmental Paper Network Paper Calculator. For more information visit www.papercalculator.org.